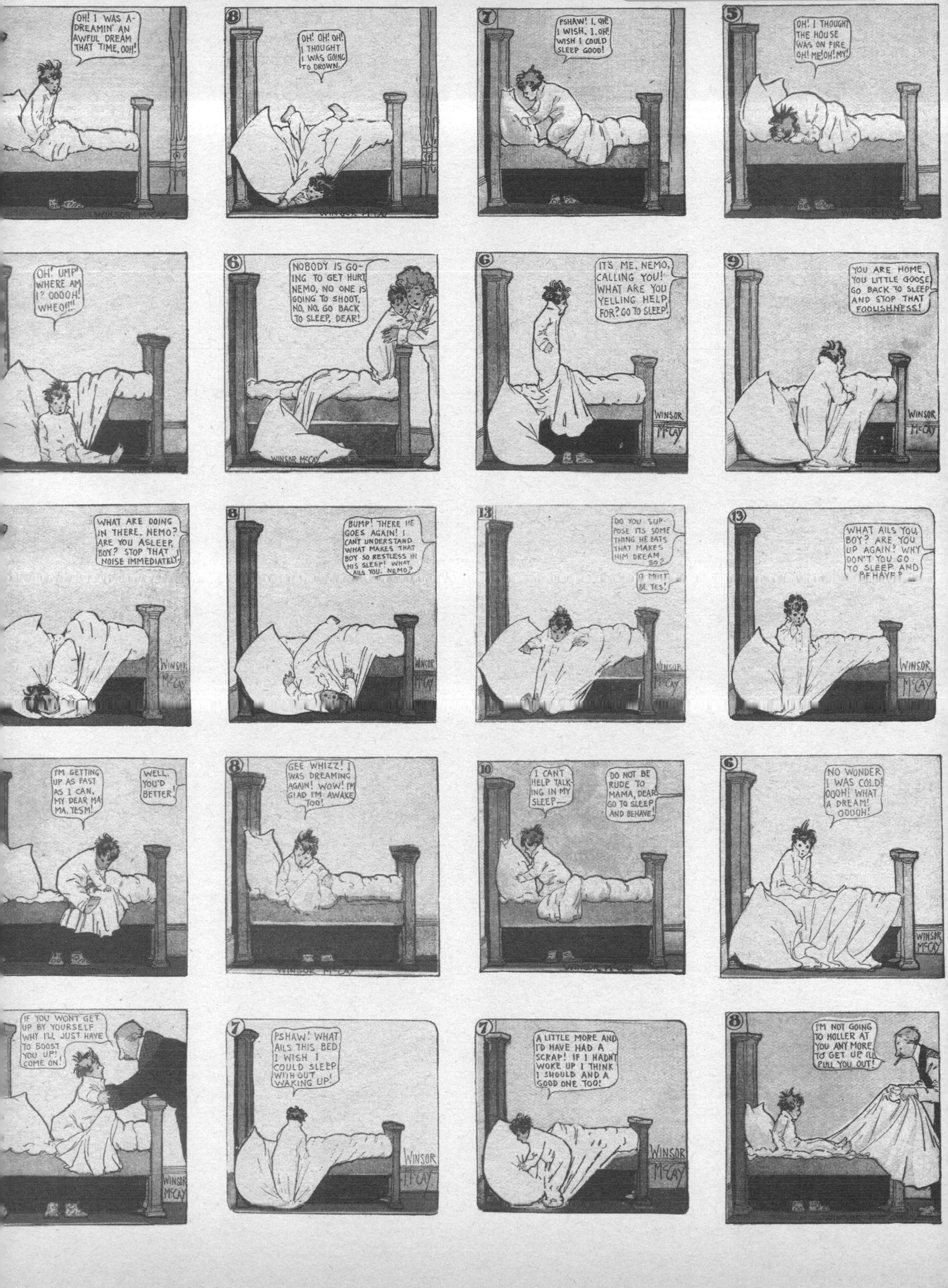

OH! I WAS A-DREAMIN' AN AWFUL DREAM THAT TIME, OOH!
WINSOR McCAY
8
OH! OH! OH! I THOUGHT I WAS GOING TO DROWN.
7
PSHAW! I, OH! I WISH, I, OH! WISH I COULD SLEEP GOOD!
5
OH! I THOUGHT THE HOUSE WAS ON FIRE OH! ME! OH! MY!
OH! UMP! WHERE AM I? OOOOH! WHEO!!!!
6
NOBODY IS GOING TO GET HURT NEMO, NO ONE IS GOING TO SHOOT, NO, NO, GO BACK TO SLEEP, DEAR!
WINSOR McCAY
6
IT'S ME, NEMO, CALLING YOU! WHAT ARE YOU YELLING HELP FOR? GO TO SLEEP!
WINSOR McCAY
9
YOU ARE HOME, YOU LITTLE GOOSE GO BACK TO SLEEP AND STOP THAT FOOLISHNESS!
WINSOR McCAY
WHAT ARE DOING IN THERE, NEMO? ARE YOU ASLEEP, BOY? STOP THAT NOISE IMMEDIATELY!
WINSOR McCAY
8
BUMP! THERE HE GOES AGAIN! I CAN'T UNDERSTAND WHAT MAKES THAT BOY SO RESTLESS IN HIS SLEEP! WHAT AILS YOU, NEMO?
13
DO YOU SUPPOSE ITS SOMETHING HE EATS THAT MAKES HIM DREAM SO?
IT MUST BE YES!
WINSOR McCAY
13
WHAT AILS YOU, BOY? ARE YOU UP AGAIN? WHY DON'T YOU GO TO SLEEP AND BEHAVE?
WINSOR McCAY
I'M GETTING UP AS FAST AS I CAN, MY DEAR MAMA. YES'M!
WELL, YOU'D BETTER!
8
GEE WHIZZ! I WAS DREAMING AGAIN! WOW! I'M GLAD I'M AWAKE TOO!
10
I CAN'T HELP TALKING IN MY SLEEP—
DO NOT BE RUDE TO MAMA, DEAR GO TO SLEEP AND BEHAVE!
6
NO WONDER I WAS COLD! OOOH! WHAT A DREAM! OOOOH!
WINSOR McCAY
IF YOU WONT GET UP BY YOURSELF WHY I'LL JUST HAVE TO BOOST YOU UP! COME ON!
WINSOR McCAY
7
PSHAW! WHAT AILS THIS BED I WISH I COULD SLEEP WITHOUT WAKING UP!
WINSOR McCAY
7
A LITTLE MORE AND I'D HAVE HAD A SCRAP! IF I HADN'T WOKE UP I THINK I SHOULD AND A GOOD ONE TOO!
WINSOR McCAY
8
I'M NOT GOING TO HOLLER AT YOU ANY MORE TO GET UP I'LL PULL YOU OUT!

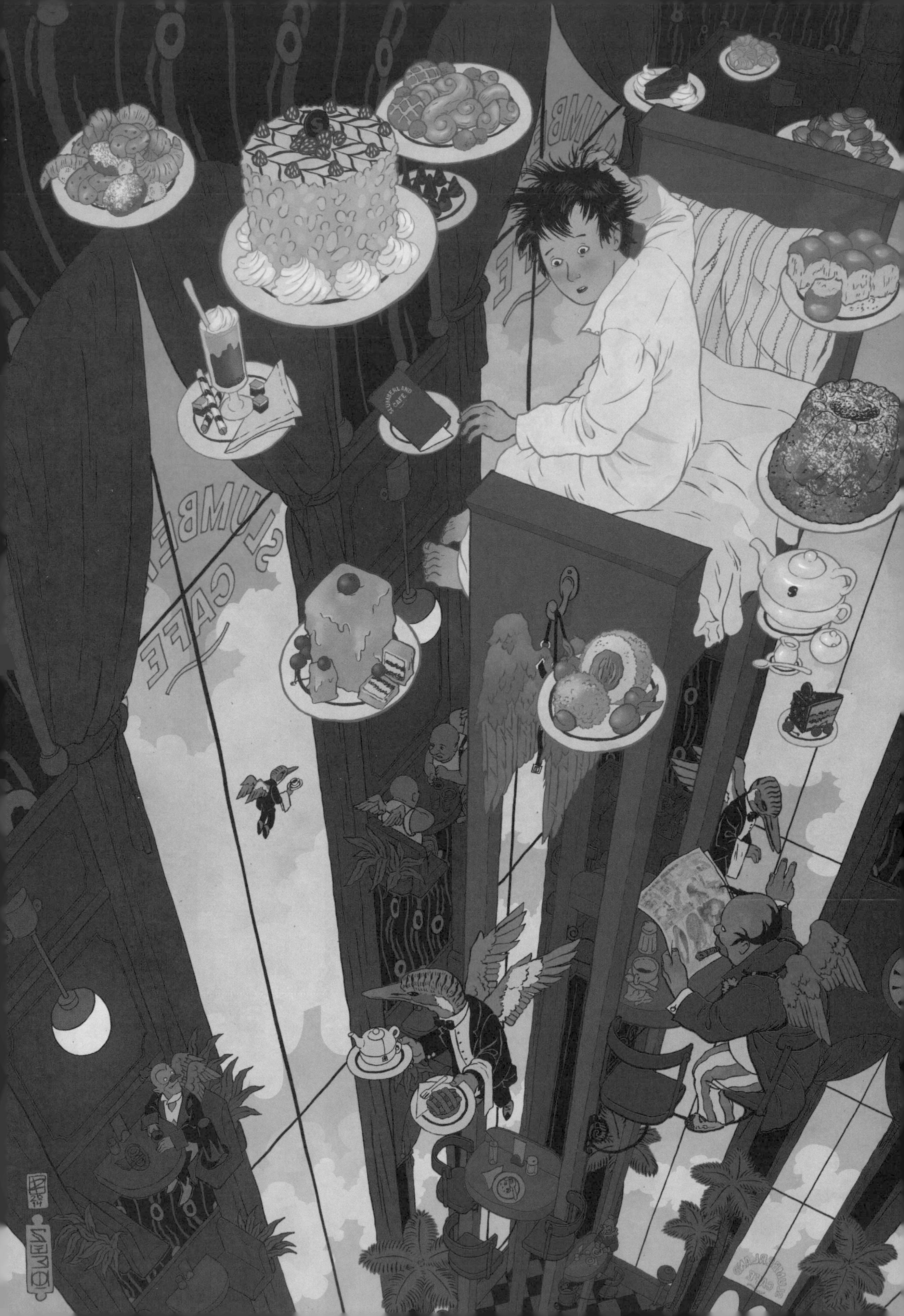

SLUMBERLAND CAFE

Little Nemo's BIG NEW DREAMS

Edited by LOCUST MOON's Josh O'Neill, Andrew Carl, and Chris Stevens

Foreword by Françoise Mouly & Art Spiegelman

JESSAMINE COUNTY PUBLIC LIBRARY
600 South Main Street
Nicholasville, KY 40356
(859) 885-3523

A TOON GRAPHIC

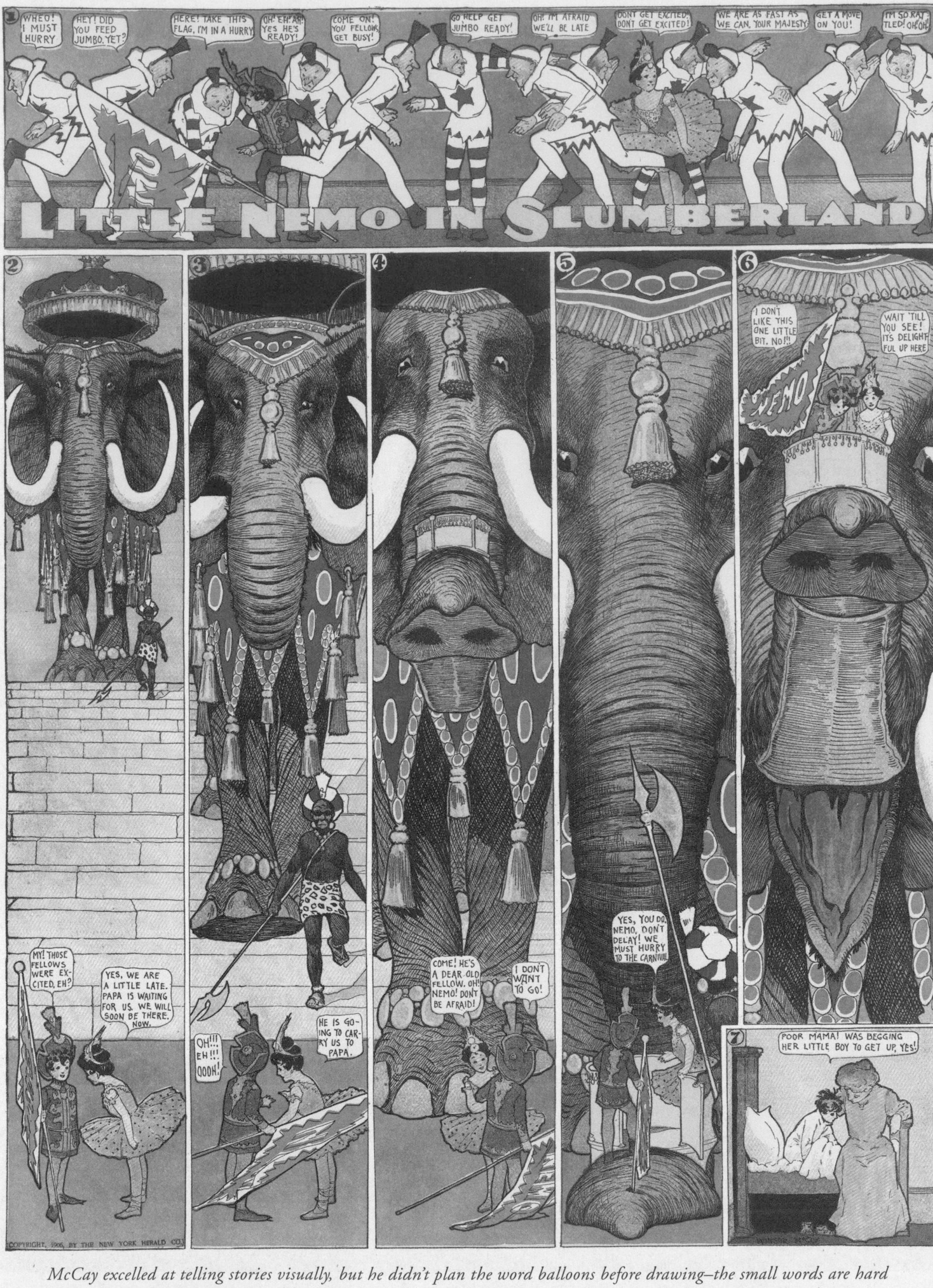
WHEO! I MUST HURRY
HEY! DID YOU FEED JUMBO, YET?
HERE! TAKE THIS FLAG, I'M IN A HURRY
OH! EH! AH! YES HE'S READY!
COME ON! YOU FELLOWS, GET BUSY!
GO HELP GET JUMBO READY!
OH! I'M AFRAID WE'LL BE LATE
DONT GET EXCITED! DONT GET EXCITED!
WE ARE AS FAST AS WE CAN, YOUR MAJESTY
GET A MOVE ON YOU!
I'M SO RAT-TLED! OH! OH!
LITTLE NEMO IN SLUMBERLAND
MY! THOSE FELLOWS WERE EX-CITED, EH?
YES, WE ARE A LITTLE LATE. PAPA IS WAITING FOR US. WE WILL SOON BE THERE. NOW.
OH!!! EH!!! OOOH!
HE IS GO-ING TO CAR-RY US TO PAPA.
COME! HE'S A DEAR OLD FELLOW. OH! NEMO! DON'T BE AFRAID!
I DON'T WANT TO GO!
YES, YOU DO, NEMO, DON'T DELAY! WE MUST HURRY TO THE CARNIVAL
I DON'T LIKE THIS ONE LITTLE BIT. NO!!!
WAIT 'TILL YOU SEE! ITS DELIGHT-FUL UP HERE
NEMO
POOR MAMA! WAS BEGGING HER LITTLE BOY TO GET UP, YES!
COPYRIGHT, 1906, BY THE NEW YORK HERALD CO.

McCay excelled at telling stories visually, but he didn't plan the word balloons before drawing–the small words are hard to read even in the large pages. The magic lies in his stunning page compositions. An elephant is not tall and narrow. It's the mark of McCay's genius that he chose to squeeze a bulky elephant marching towards Nemo, the Princess, and the reader into tall and narrow panels.

SEEING THE WORLD THROUGH COMICS...

by Françoise Mouly

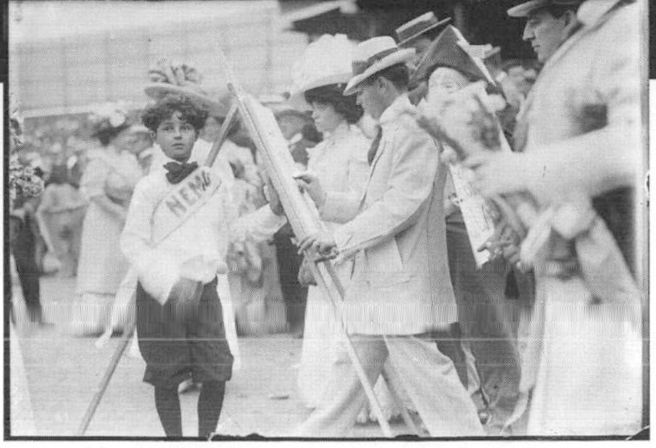

Winsor McCay at the easel drawing his son Robert, the model for Little Nemo.

To see a Winsor McCay page is to read it. The experience is vivid and immediately engrossing. Just glance at the page on the left, and the elephant jumps out at you. You nearly want to step out of the way of that advancing trunk.

I first experienced the magic of those early newspaper pages upon my arrival in New York, as a young adult in the late 1970s. I had a hard time speaking and understanding English, having grown up in France, and I sought out comics, thinking that they would offer me a point of entry into American culture. I soon discovered that in the U.S. at that time, comics were neither readily available nor taken very seriously. But I had the (immense) good fortune of being introduced to a young cartoonist named Art Spiegelman. Although he hadn't yet started the work he's now famous for, the graphic novel *Maus*, Art was already a passionate advocate for his medium. And he, for his part, was pleased to come across someone actually asking for comics. He wooed and courted me by pulling giant newspaper sheets awash with gorgeous color, pages of *Little Nemo*, out of his closet. Soon I was falling in love–with Art, with McCay's creation, and with comics in general. "Why weren't these on every newsstand and in every bookstore?" I wanted to know. "Why did these luscious pages exist only in his closet?" Art gave me a brief history lesson. He explained that comics had once been a hugely popular medium. Comic books sold millions of copies every week, and ninety-four percent of all American children read them regularly. Then, in the 50s, a psychologist named Dr. Fredric Wertham went on a campaign to decry the rather gruesome horror comics that were popular at the time, saying they caused juvenile delinquency. He stirred the public's outrage, which led to book burnings and, in 1954, Congressional hearings. And after that, comics pretty much disappeared.

At the time I met him, Art was one of a handful of underground cartoonists who were eager to give new life to the medium by using it for personal expression. Art himself had discovered McCay through a mentor, Woody Gelman, an ex-animator with a love of and vision for the work, who had collected the fragile newspaper pages. Gelman also salvaged the original drawings when he saw that McCay's son, Robert, an unsuccessful artist, was using them as boards to protect the drawing tables in his studio.

Little Nemo has been an inspiration to me since the day I discovered it and an integral part of the great loves of my life. When Art and I decided to publish a comics magazine, *RAW*, in the early 80s, we featured work by McCay in the first issue. I hauled a printing press up to our fourth-floor loft, and I felt I was sharing in McCay's giddiness, creating art with the cyan (blue), magenta (red), yellow, and black inks that offset printing presses still use to reproduce color today. Around the time our first child was born, Art did a review in comic book form for a biography of McCay. (I adapted it for this book, and it is reproduced overleaf. I'm the girl mouse in the last panel.) At bedtime, our kids got to meet King Morpheus, the kind and patient Princess, and the sharp-tongued Flip–the characters infiltrated their own dreams. We had to discuss with them the portrayal of the Jungle Imp, a black character who is unfortunately drawn in a way typical of the early twentieth century's colonial legacy. (Cliff Chiang tackles the issue with tact on page 25: "How silly..." says a boy holding a mask that looks like the Imp.)

Over the years, McCay's pages have finally been reprinted in beautiful hardcover books. It brings me great joy to see that what was once a fragile set of folded newspaper pages tucked away in a closet is being discovered by new generations.

And when the editors of Locust Moon showed me the resplendent comics that contemporary artists were producing as an homage to McCay's creation, I wanted to publish this book. Once you fall into Slumberland, it's hard to leave it. But now, thanks to some of today's foremost cartoonists, you and I can turn page after page and start dreaming all over again.

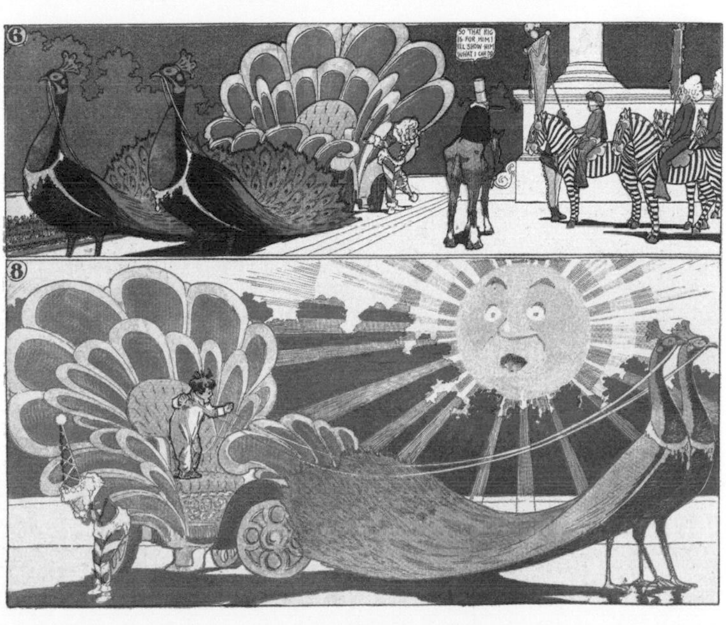
6
SO THAT RIG IS FOR HIM! I'LL SHOW HIM WHAT I CAN DO
8

Françoise Mouly is the Editorial Director of TOON Books as well as the Art Editor of The New Yorker. *Art Spiegelman is the author of the Pulitzer Prize-winning* Maus, A Survivor's Tale, *and many other books.*

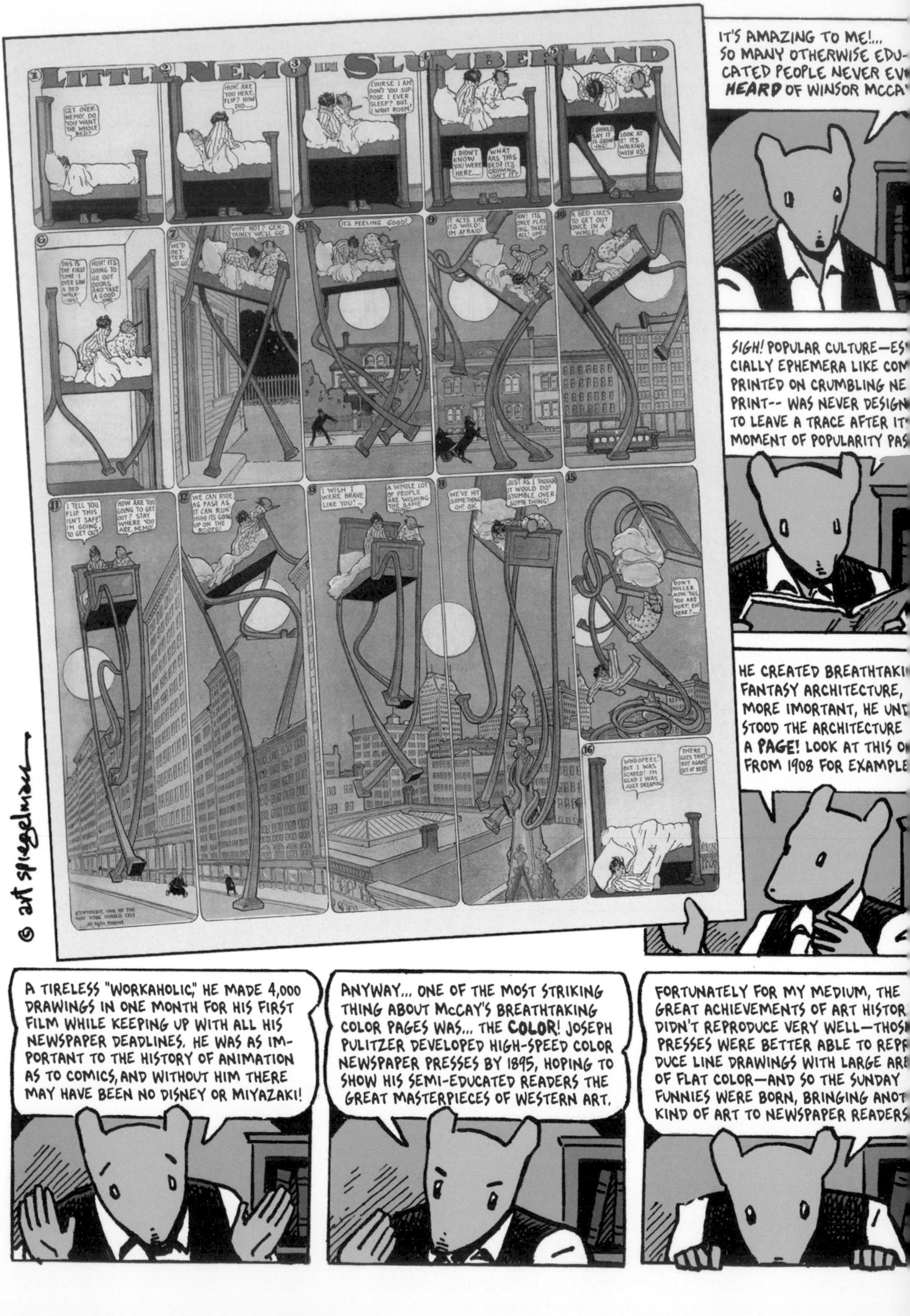
LITTLE NEMO IN SLUMBERLAND
GET OVER, NEMO! DO YOU WANT THE WHOLE BED?
HUH! ARE YOU HERE, FLIP? HOW DID....
COURSE I AM! DON'T YOU SUPPOSE I EVER SLEEP? BUT I WANT ROOM!
I DIDN'T KNOW YOU WERE HERE....
WHAT AILS THIS BED? ITS GROWING, ISN'T IT?
I SHOULD SAY IT IS GROWING!
LOOK AT IT! ITS WALKING WITH US!
THIS IS THE FIRST TIME I EVER SAW A BED WALKING!
HUH! ITS GOING TO GO OUT DOORS AND TAKE A GOOD ONE!
WE'D BETTER NOT GO!
WHY NOT? CERTAINLY WE'LL GO!
ITS FEELING GOOD!
IT ACTS LIKE ITS WILD! I'M AFRAID!
AW! ITS ONLY PLAYING, THAT'S ALL! UM!
A BED LIKES TO GET OUT ONCE IN A WHILE!
I TELL YOU FLIP THIS ISN'T SAFE! I'M GOING TO GET OUT!
HOW ARE YOU GOING TO GET OUT? STAY WHERE YOU ARE, NEMO!
WE CAN RIDE AS FAST AS IT CAN RUN! HUH! ITS GOING UP ON THE ROOFS!
I WISH I WERE BRAVE LIKE YOU!
A WHOLE LOT OF PEOPLE ARE WISHING THE SAME THING!
WE'VE HIT SOMETHING! OH! OH!
JUST AS I THOUGHT IT WOULD DO! STUMBLE OVER SOMETHING!
WHOOPEE! BUT I WAS SCARED! I'M GLAD I WAS JUST DREAMING!
THERE GOES THAT BOY AGAIN OUT OF BED!
IT'S AMAZING TO ME!... SO MANY OTHERWISE EDU-CATED PEOPLE NEVER EV HEARD OF WINSOR MCCA
SIGH! POPULAR CULTURE—ES CIALLY EPHEMERA LIKE COM PRINTED ON CRUMBLING NE PRINT-- WAS NEVER DESIGN TO LEAVE A TRACE AFTER IT MOMENT OF POPULARITY PAS
HE CREATED BREATHTAKI FANTASY ARCHITECTURE, MORE IMORTANT, HE UND STOOD THE ARCHITECTURE A PAGE! LOOK AT THIS O FROM 1908 FOR EXAMPLE
A TIRELESS "WORKAHOLIC," HE MADE 4,000 DRAWINGS IN ONE MONTH FOR HIS FIRST FILM WHILE KEEPING UP WITH ALL HIS NEWSPAPER DEADLINES. HE WAS AS IM-PORTANT TO THE HISTORY OF ANIMATION AS TO COMICS, AND WITHOUT HIM THERE MAY HAVE BEEN NO DISNEY OR MIYAZAKI!
ANYWAY... ONE OF THE MOST STRIKING THING ABOUT McCAY'S BREATHTAKING COLOR PAGES WAS... THE COLOR! JOSEPH PULITZER DEVELOPED HIGH-SPEED COLOR NEWSPAPER PRESSES BY 1895, HOPING TO SHOW HIS SEMI-EDUCATED READERS THE GREAT MASTERPIECES OF WESTERN ART.
FORTUNATELY FOR MY MEDIUM, THE GREAT ACHIEVEMENTS OF ART HISTOR DIDN'T REPRODUCE VERY WELL—THOS PRESSES WERE BETTER ABLE TO REP DUCE LINE DRAWINGS WITH LARGE AR OF FLAT COLOR—AND SO THE SUNDAY FUNNIES WERE BORN, BRINGING ANOT KIND OF ART TO NEWSPAPER READERS
© art spiegelman

...NO WAS A SUCCESS IN 1905, BUT BY THE [MID]DLE OF THE 20TH CENTURY, WINSOR McC[AY']S FANTASY MASTERPIECE WAS TOTALLY *FORGOTTEN!*

IT STARTED AS AN "UPSCALE" FEATURE IN THE NEW YORK HERALD'S WEEKLY COLOR COMICS SECTION...

THE VERY FIRST POPULAR COMICS—THE YELLOW KID, THE KATZENJAMMERS, HAPPY HOOLIGAN—WERE RAUCOUS VAUDEVILLE SLAPSTICK. NEMO BROUGHT COMICS OUT OF THE CITY'S SLUMS AND INTO THE PARLOR!

...OUR CULTURE THRIVES ON THE VITAL [WAR] OF WAR BETWEEN THE VULGAR AND [TH]E GENTEEL. BOTH TENDENCIES FEED [EAC]H OTHER, SO TODAY IT'S *EASY* TO CON[CLU]DE THAT COMICS ARE AN ART FORM,...

AND THAT McCAY WAS A MASTER OF THE NEW MEDIUM, CONVINCINGLY MAPPING OUT THE MIND'S INNER DREAMSCAPE DECADES BEFORE ANY SURREALIST DRAPED A MELTING CLOCK ON THE LIMB OF A TREE!

McCAY WAS A REMARKABLE DRAFTSMAN, PROLIFIC AND *FAST!* (ON THE VAUDEVILLE STAGE HE'D PRODUCE 25 DRAWINGS IN 15 MINUTES!) HE HAD AN UNCANNY FEEL FOR MOVEMENT, PERSPECTIVE AND PAGEANTRY, AND HE UNDERSTOOD THE COMICS FORM...

...LOOK AT HOW THE ROWS OF PANELS [STRE]TCH TO ACCOMMODATE THE GROWING [BED] AS IT CANTERS INTO AND OVER THE [...] AND LOOK AT HOW THE MOON [DA]NCES IN RHYTHMIC COUNTERPOINT [TO T]HE BED'S SINUOUS MOVEMENTS...

AND LOOK AT HOW THE MOON JOINS TWO PANELS INTO ONE AS THE BED STUMBLES OVER A CHURCH STEEPLE. AND LOOK AT HOW NEMO FLOATS DOWN THAT LAST NARROW VERTICAL BOX TO LAND, AS ALWAYS, IN THAT SMALL BOX OF A BEDROOM. *THE GUY WAS A GENIUS!*

FROM THIS PAGE ALONE YOU CAN BE SURE HE STUDIED MUYBRIDGE'S 19TH CENTURY ANIMAL LOCOMOTION PHOTOGRAPHS—AND AFTER SEEING HIS SON'S FLIPBOOKS, HE GOT INTERESTED IN SEEING HIS OWN DRAWINGS MOVE. HE EXPLORED AND REDEFINED THE NEWBORN ART OF ANIMATED CARTOONS...

...PRINTERS WERE AS EXCITED BY COLOR [REP]RODUCTION AS THE ARTISTS. McCAY [WOR]KED *ESPECIALLY* CLOSELY WITH THE [PRE]SSMEN AT THE NY HERALD, REPUTED [TO H]AVE THE BEST PRESSES AT THAT TIME, [LOOK], FOR EXAMPLE, AT THE NEXT SPREAD, [A]T THE SUMPTUOUS DETAIL ON THE [PREV]IOUS PAGE, WITH THE BLACK OUTLINES [PRIN]TED TO THE BLUE PLATE, AS SLUMBERLAND FADES WHEN DAWN ARRIVES. WOW!

Y'KNOW, NOW THAT WE'RE IN THE DIGITAL AGE WE HEAR MORE AND MORE ABOUT THE "DEATH OF THE BOOK," BUT IT'S IRONIC THAT THE MOST BEAUTIFUL BOOKS SINCE THE INVENTION OF PRINTING ARE MADE POSSIBLE TODAY THANKS TO THE SAME TECHNOLOGY THAT THREATENS TO REPLACE THEM,... AND I ASSURE YOU THESE NEMO PAGES WON'T LOOK LIKE MUCH ON YOUR IPHONE OR IPAD!

WHEEOO! I DREAMED THERE WAS A NEW BOOK OF CARTOONISTS' HOMAGES TO *LITTLE NEMO* AND—FOR SOME REASON—I HAD TO WRITE A FOREWORD IN COMICS FORM,... BUT I GOT CRUSHED BY MY SPEECH BALLOON!

HMMPH! NO MORE PEPPERONI PIZZAS FOR *YOU* BEFORE BEDTIME.

The original version of Art Spiegelman's foreword was published in USA Today in 1987 as a review of John Canemaker's *Winsor McCay: His Life and Art.*

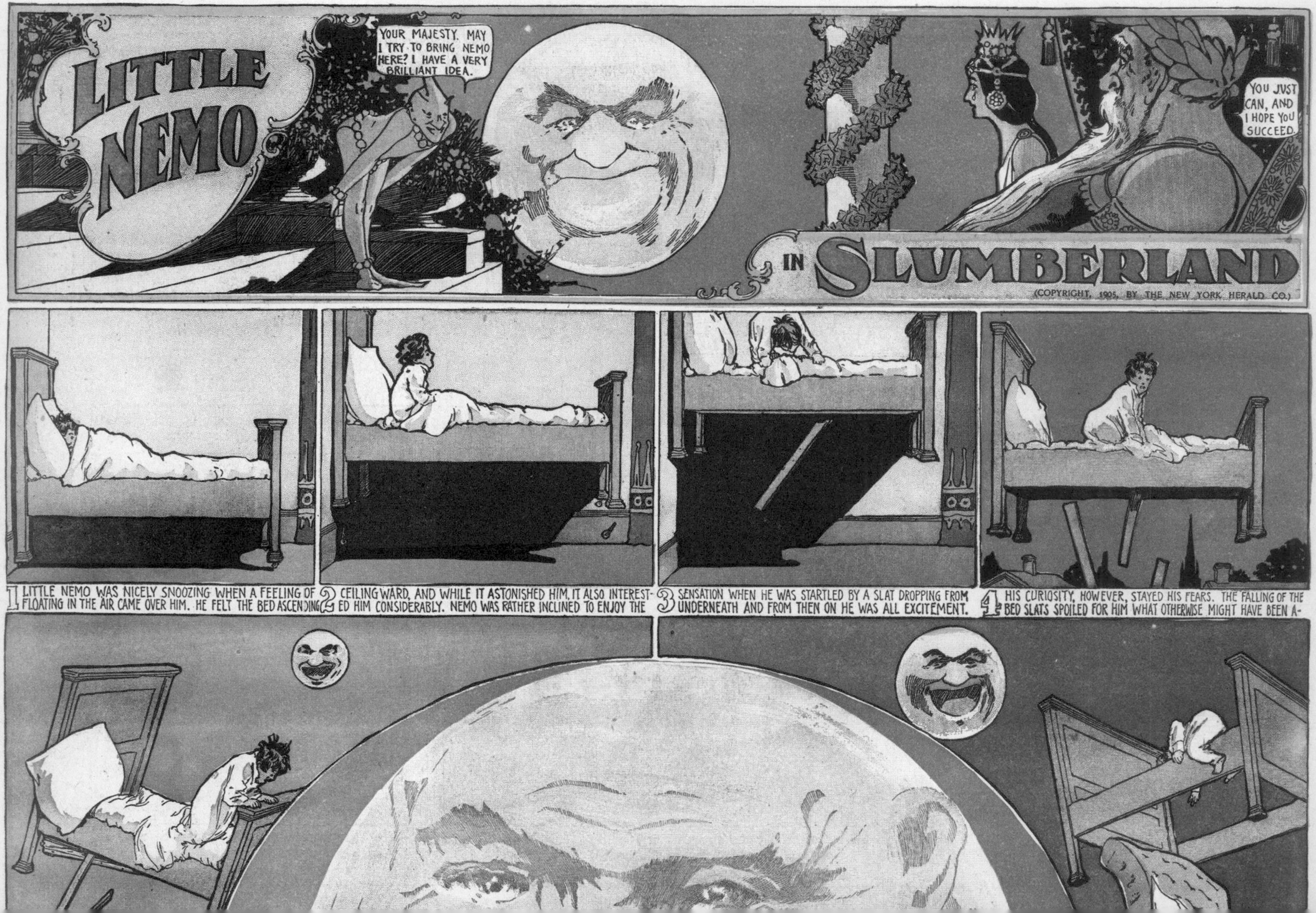
LITTLE NEMO IN SLUMBERLAND
(COPYRIGHT, 1905, BY THE NEW YORK HERALD CO.)
YOUR MAJESTY. MAY I TRY TO BRING NEMO HERE? I HAVE A VERY BRILLIANT IDEA.
YOU JUST CAN, AND I HOPE YOU SUCCEED.
1 LITTLE NEMO WAS NICELY SNOOZING WHEN A FEELING OF FLOATING IN THE AIR CAME OVER HIM. HE FELT THE BED ASCENDING
2 CEILINGWARD, AND WHILE IT ASTONISHED HIM, IT ALSO INTERESTED HIM CONSIDERABLY. NEMO WAS RATHER INCLINED TO ENJOY THE
3 SENSATION WHEN HE WAS STARTLED BY A SLAT DROPPING FROM UNDERNEATH AND FROM THEN ON HE WAS ALL EXCITEMENT.
4 HIS CURIOSITY, HOWEVER, STAYED HIS FEARS. THE FALLING OF THE BED SLATS SPOILED FOR HIM WHAT OTHERWISE MIGHT HAVE BEEN A-

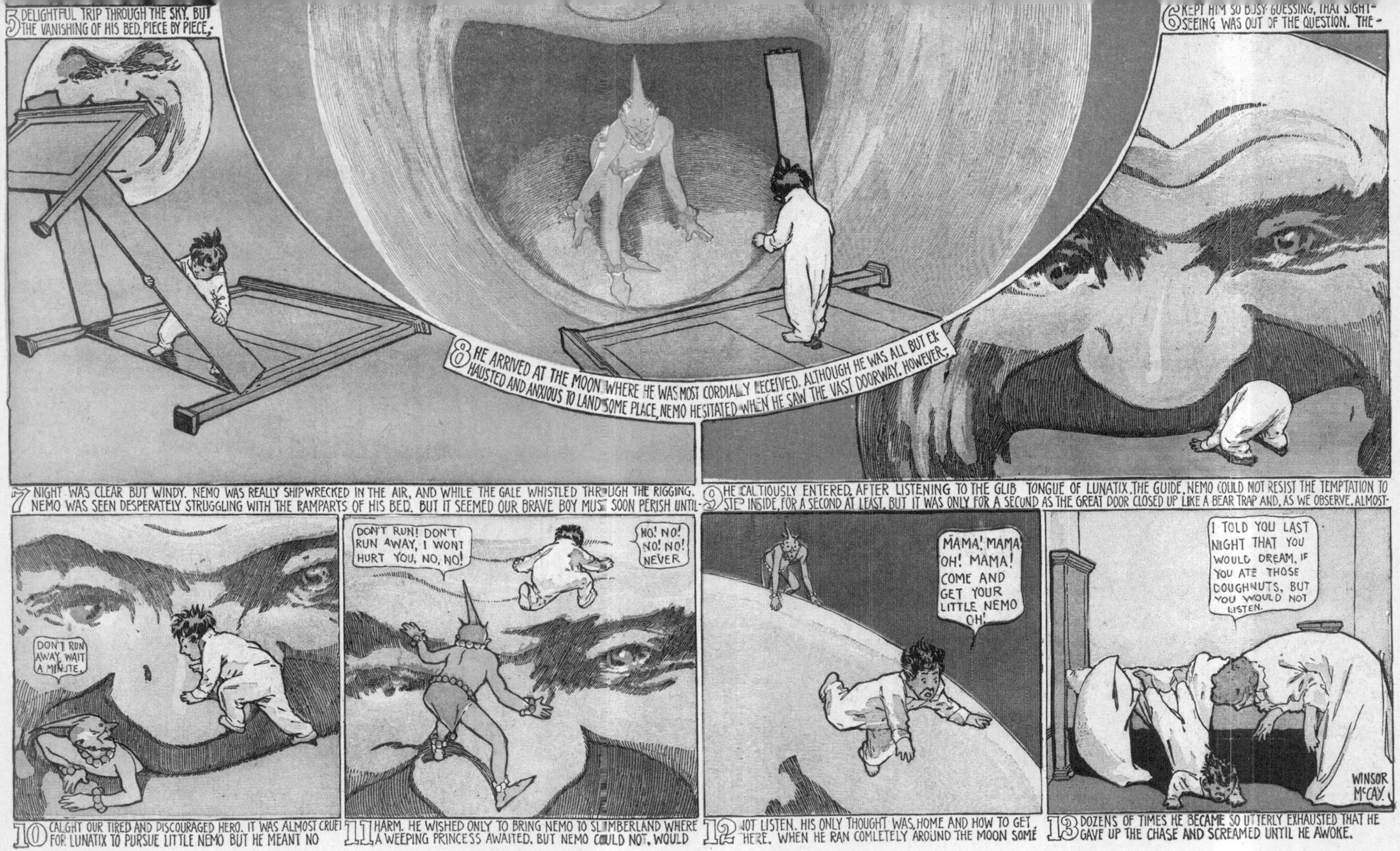
5 DELIGHTFUL TRIP THROUGH THE SKY, BUT THE VANISHING OF HIS BED, PIECE BY PIECE,-
6 KEPT HIM SO BUSY GUESSING, THAT SIGHT-SEEING WAS OUT OF THE QUESTION. THE-
8 HE ARRIVED AT THE MOON WHERE HE WAS MOST CORDIALLY RECEIVED. ALTHOUGH HE WAS ALL BUT EXHAUSTED AND ANXIOUS TO LAND SOME PLACE, NEMO HESITATED WHEN HE SAW THE VAST DOORWAY. HOWEVER,-
7 NIGHT WAS CLEAR BUT WINDY. NEMO WAS REALLY SHIPWRECKED IN THE AIR, AND WHILE THE GALE WHISTLED THROUGH THE RIGGING, NEMO WAS SEEN DESPERATELY STRUGGLING WITH THE RAMPARTS OF HIS BED. BUT IT SEEMED OUR BRAVE BOY MUST SOON PERISH UNTIL-
9 HE CAUTIOUSLY ENTERED. AFTER LISTENING TO THE GLIB TONGUE OF LUNATIX, THE GUIDE, NEMO COULD NOT RESIST THE TEMPTATION TO STEP INSIDE, FOR A SECOND AT LEAST, BUT IT WAS ONLY FOR A SECOND AS THE GREAT DOOR CLOSED UP LIKE A BEAR TRAP AND, AS WE OBSERVE, ALMOST-
DON'T RUN AWAY, WAIT A MINUTE.
DON'T RUN! DON'T RUN AWAY, I WONT HURT YOU, NO, NO!
NO! NO! NO! NO! NEVER
MAMA! MAMA! OH! MAMA! COME AND GET YOUR LITTLE NEMO OH!
I TOLD YOU LAST NIGHT THAT YOU WOULD DREAM, IF YOU ATE THOSE DOUGHNUTS, BUT YOU WOULD NOT LISTEN.
WINSOR McCAY.
10 CAUGHT OUR TIRED AND DISCOURAGED HERO. IT WAS ALMOST CRUEL FOR LUNATIX TO PURSUE LITTLE NEMO BUT HE MEANT NO
11 HARM. HE WISHED ONLY TO BRING NEMO TO SLUMBERLAND WHERE A WEEPING PRINCESS AWAITED. BUT NEMO COULD NOT, WOULD
12 NOT LISTEN. HIS ONLY THOUGHT WAS, HOME AND HOW TO GET THERE. WHEN HE RAN COMLETELY AROUND THE MOON SOME
13 DOZENS OF TIMES HE BECAME SO UTTERLY EXHAUSTED THAT HE GAVE UP THE CHASE AND SCREAMED UNTIL HE AWOKE.

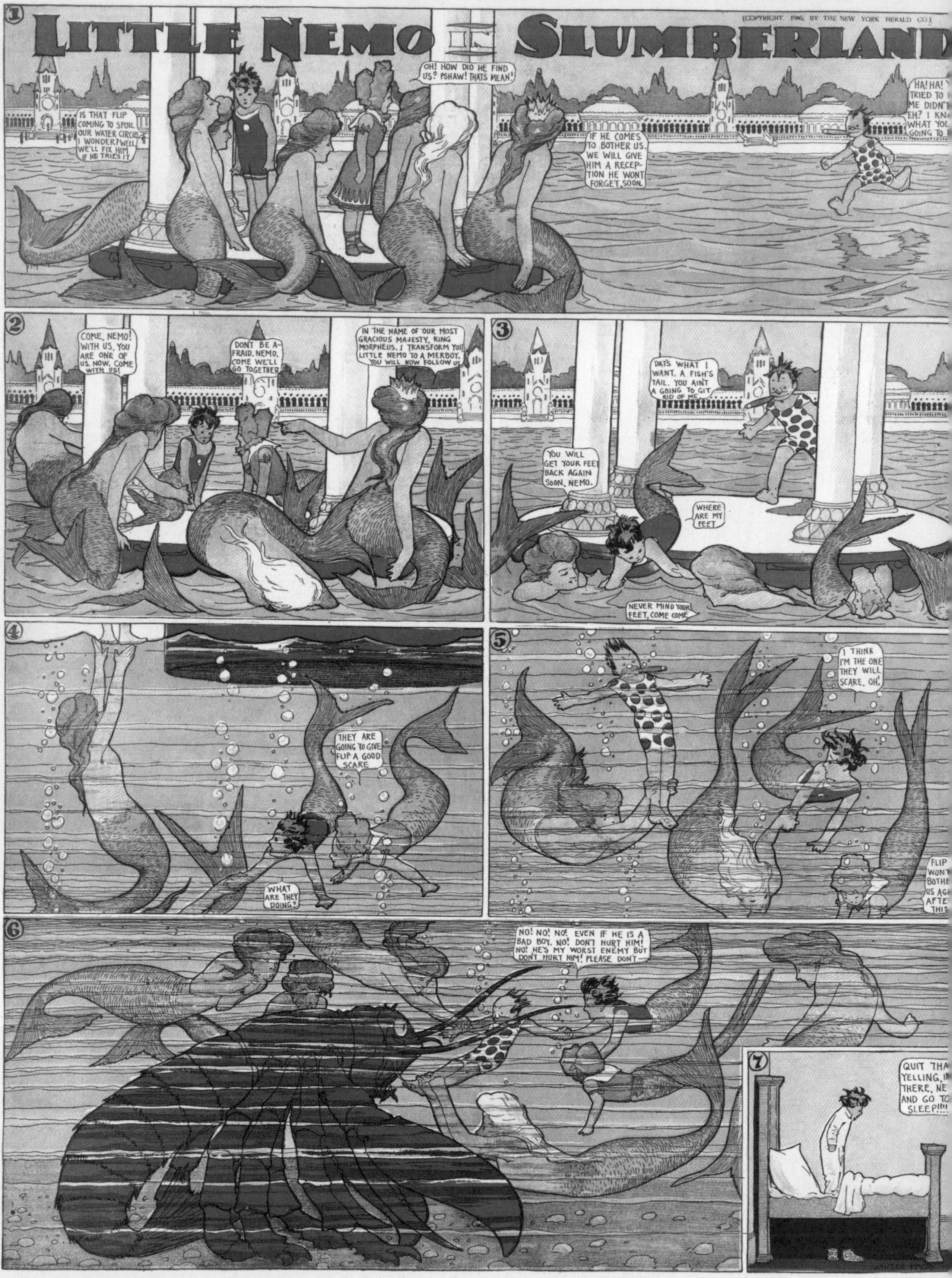
LITTLE NEMO IN SLUMBERLAND
(COPYRIGHT. 1906, BY THE NEW YORK HERALD CO.)
IS THAT FLIP COMING TO SPOIL OUR WATER CIRCUS I WONDER? WELL WE'LL FIX HIM IF HE TRIES IT
OH! HOW DID HE FIND US? PSHAW! THAT'S MEAN!
IF HE COMES TO BOTHER US. WE WILL GIVE HIM A RECEPTION HE WONT FORGET SOON.
HA! HA! TRIED TO ME DIDN'T EH? I KNO WHAT YOU GOING TO
COME, NEMO! WITH US, YOU ARE ONE OF US, NOW. COME WITH US!
DONT BE AFRAID, NEMO, COME WE'LL GO TOGETHER
IN THE NAME OF OUR MOST GRACIOUS MAJESTY, KING MORPHEUS, I TRANSFORM YOU LITTLE NEMO TO A MERBOY. YOU WILL NOW FOLLOW US
DAT'S WHAT I WANT. A FISH'S TAIL. YOU AINT A GOING TO GIT RID OF ME.
YOU WILL GET YOUR FEET BACK AGAIN SOON, NEMO.
WHERE ARE MY FEET
NEVER MIND YOUR FEET, COME COME
THEY ARE GOING TO GIVE FLIP A GOOD SCARE
WHAT ARE THEY DOING?
I THINK I'M THE ONE THEY WILL SCARE. OH!
NO! NO! NO! EVEN IF HE IS A BAD BOY, NO! DONT HURT HIM! NO! HE'S MY WORST ENEMY BUT DONT HURT HIM! PLEASE DON'T
QUIT THA YELLING, IN THERE, NE AND GO TO SLEEP!!!!

CELEBRATING LITTLE NEMO

by LOCUST MOON's Josh O'Neill, Andrew Carl, and Chris Stevens

The book you hold in your hands is a secret treasure smuggled out of Slumberland under the darkness of sleep. Folded like a collection of letters waiting to be opened by a reader, here are thirty-one new dreams inspired by a work from a century ago. Winsor McCay's Little Nemo in Slumberland *is brought back through the strange and delicate antennae of some of the most imaginative artists working today. Here's the story of how this book came into being.*

To this day, the Little Nemo comic strips by Winsor McCay stand as a singular achievement in modern art. But even though McCay's work continues to resonate through the two art forms he pioneered, comics and animation, McCay and his work are still not well known to large segments of the public. So, back in 2012, we at Locust Moon Press began working on *Little Nemo: Dream Another Dream*, an anthology in which over a hundred contemporary cartoonists would pay tribute to the master and his masterpiece with brand-new Little Nemo strips of their own.

Early newspapers were printed on 16" by 21" broadsheets, about four times bigger than this book. We had admired Sunday Press' reprints of early strips recently reissued at original size and decided we should give our artists the same glorious broadsheet page as their canvas. The project quickly took on a life of its own, and before long it seemed that the entire comics community had united behind it. But our mission to spread McCay's glory to a wider audience couldn't end with an oversized art book. Now, together with Françoise Mouly and the team at TOON Books, themselves makers of transcendent children's books and young adult comics, we are able to present this abridged collection: thirty-one carefully selected works out of the hundred and eighteen originally commissioned. Our hope is that this compact edition, appropriate for bookshelves in every home, school, and library, will allow everyone the opportunity to own a piece of the dream.

Little NEMO
DREAM ANOTHER DREAM

In these pages you will find an echo of the myriad tropes of Winsor McCay's formidable imagination. The ice palaces, the noble elephants, the mind-melting circuses and the funhouse mirrors, the oomps and gumps and smiling moons, the golden spires that twist ever upward, the silly, glorious pomp and pageantry of the slumbering kingdom–they're all here, reinterpreted through the talents of new cartoonists. But you'll see that no matter where the dream takes Nemo, the artists always return our boy to his bed, his adventures abruptly interrupted, and have him land back where he started, safe and sound. Because for all the fearlessness and creativity on display, these contemporary storymakers are also keepers of McCay's enduring tradition.

You can hear McCay's footsteps echoing through these corridors, where his spiritual heirs stand sentry. Our mission is to spread this gospel far and wide–we think that Slumberland belongs to everyone. Maybe you, reader, will make your own Little Nemo comic strip!

The great, befuddling halls of Slumberland will wind on forever. Walk them with us. Let's see where they lead.

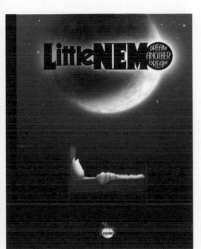

Josh O'Neill, Andrew Carl, and Chris Stevens, run Locust Moon, a comics publisher and store in Philadelphia. The Locust Moon edition, Little Nemo: Dream Another Dream, *features one hundred and eighteen contributors, measures 16" x 21" and weighs nearly 10 pounds.*

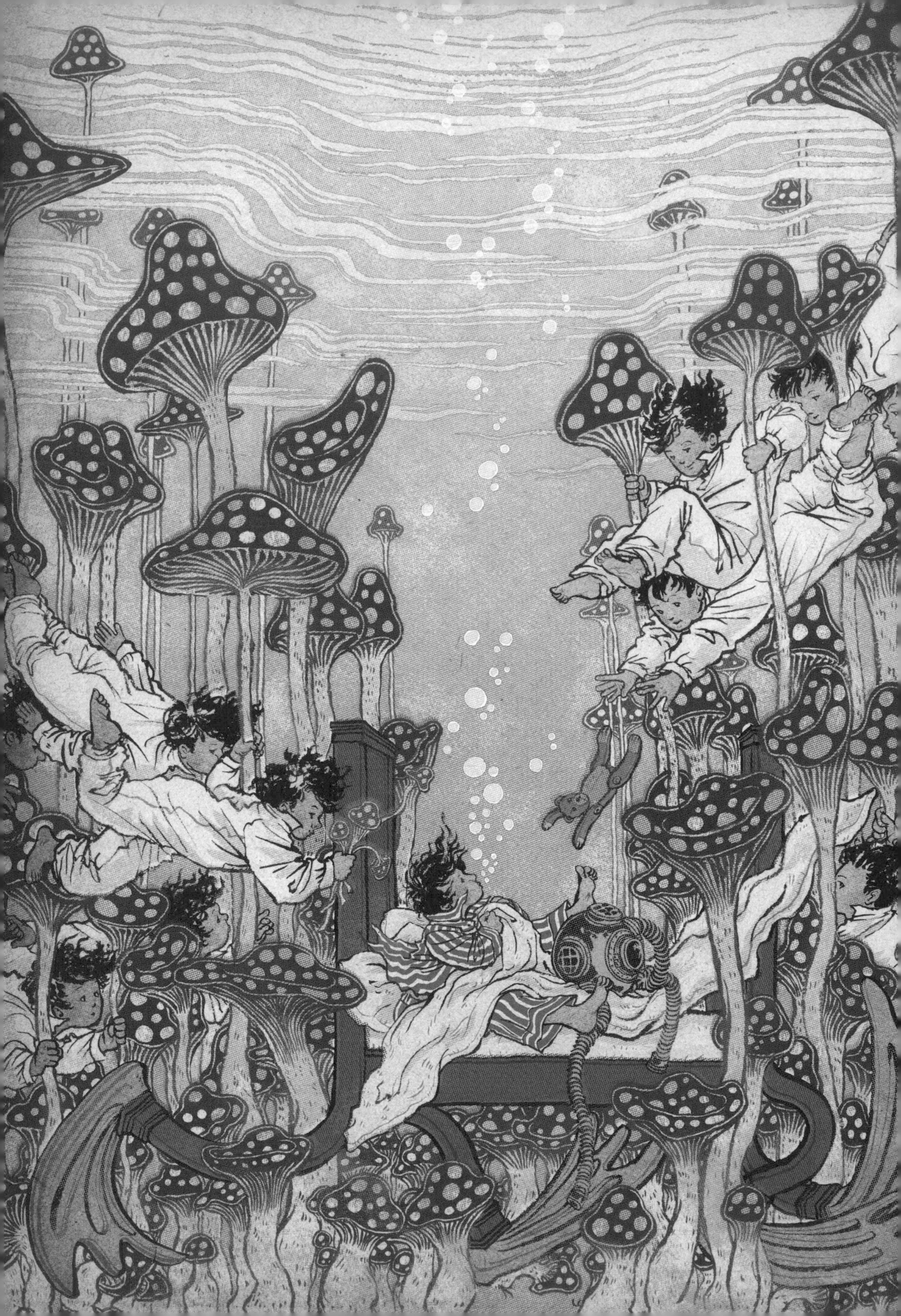

Little Nemo's
BIG NEW DREAMS

COVERS

Front top panel: Roger Langridge
Front bottom panel: Charles Vess
Back cover: Gerhard

4   Peter Diamond

5   *(Title page)* Mark Buckingham, colored by D'Israeli

14 *(Facing this page)* Yuko Shimizu

17 Roger Langridge

19 Peter Hoey and Maria Hoey

21 Paolo Rivera

23 Carla Speed McNeil

25 Cliff Chiang

27 Zander Cannon

29 Craig Thompson

31 James Harvey

33 David Mack

35 Cole Closser

37 Jeremy Bastian

39 David Petersen

41 Jamie Tanner

43 Nik Poliwko

45 David Plunkert

47 Aaron Conley

49 Bishakh Kumar Som

51 Maris Wicks & Joe Quinones

53 Box Brown

55 Andrea Tsurumi

57 R. Sikoryak

59 Hans Rickheit

61 Marc Hempel

62 James Yang

63 J.G. Jones, *colored by* José Villarrubia

66 Jim Rugg

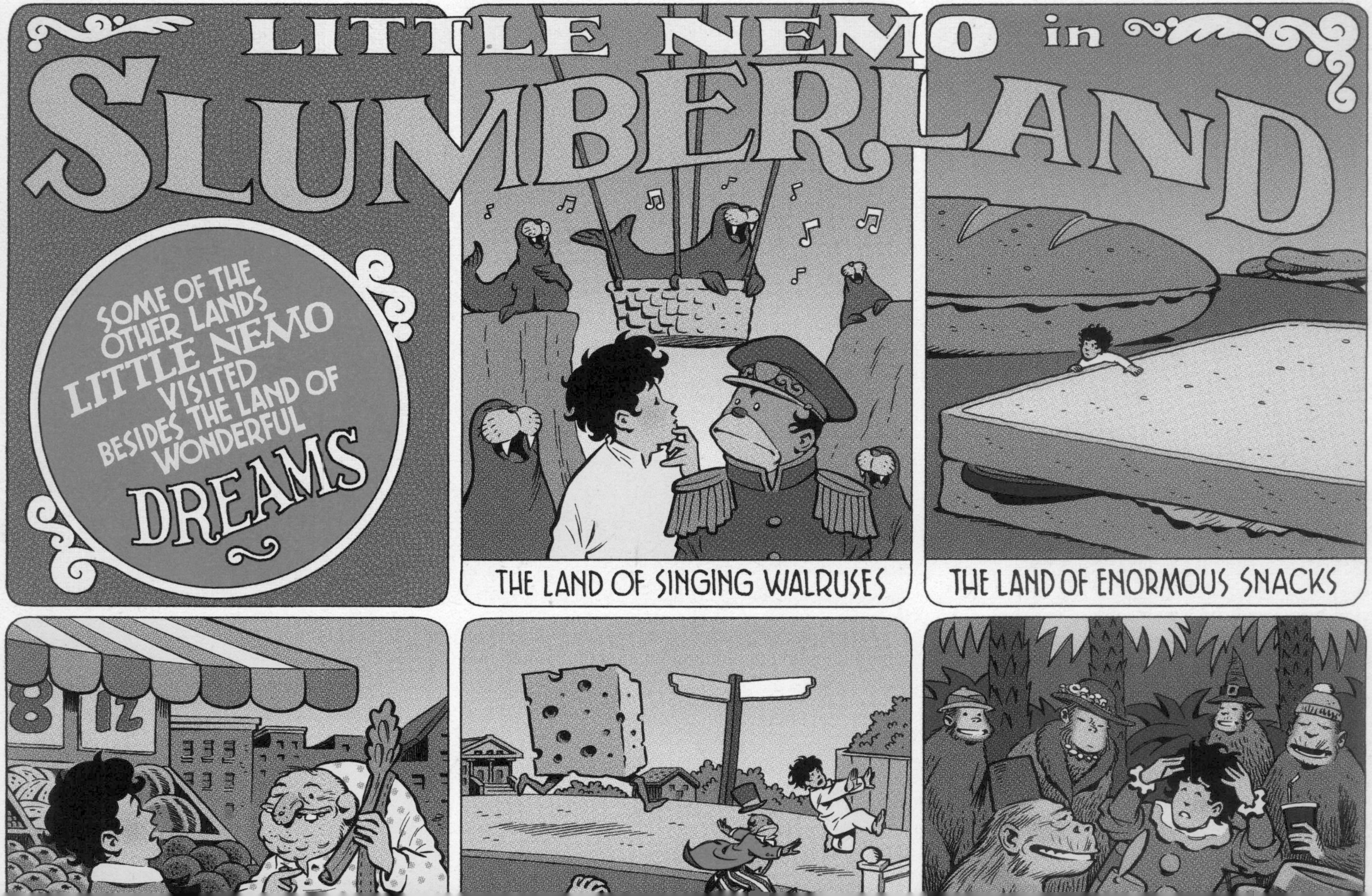
LITTLE NEMO in SLUMBERLAND
SOME OF THE OTHER LANDS LITTLE NEMO VISITED BESIDES THE LAND OF WONDERFUL DREAMS
THE LAND OF SINGING WALRUSES
THE LAND OF ENORMOUS SNACKS
8 12

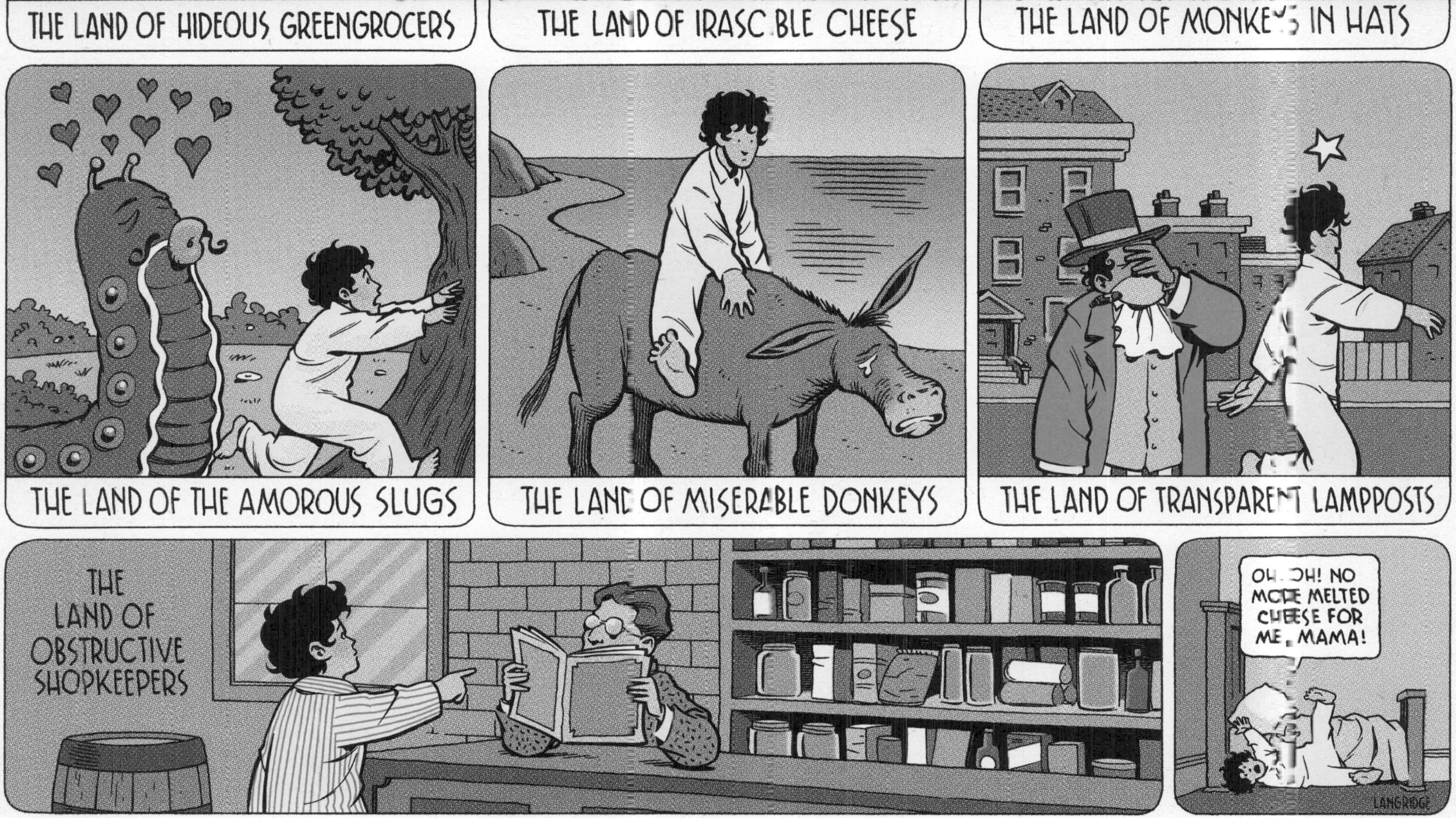
THE LAND OF HIDEOUS GREENGROCERS
THE LAND OF IRASCIBLE CHEESE
THE LAND OF MONKEYS IN HATS
THE LAND OF THE AMOROUS SLUGS
THE LAND OF MISERABLE DONKEYS
THE LAND OF TRANSPARENT LAMPPOSTS
THE LAND OF OBSTRUCTIVE SHOPKEEPERS
OH-OH! NO MORE MELTED CHEESE FOR ME, MAMA!
LANGRIDGE

Roger Langridge

LITTLE NEMO IN COIN-OP LAND

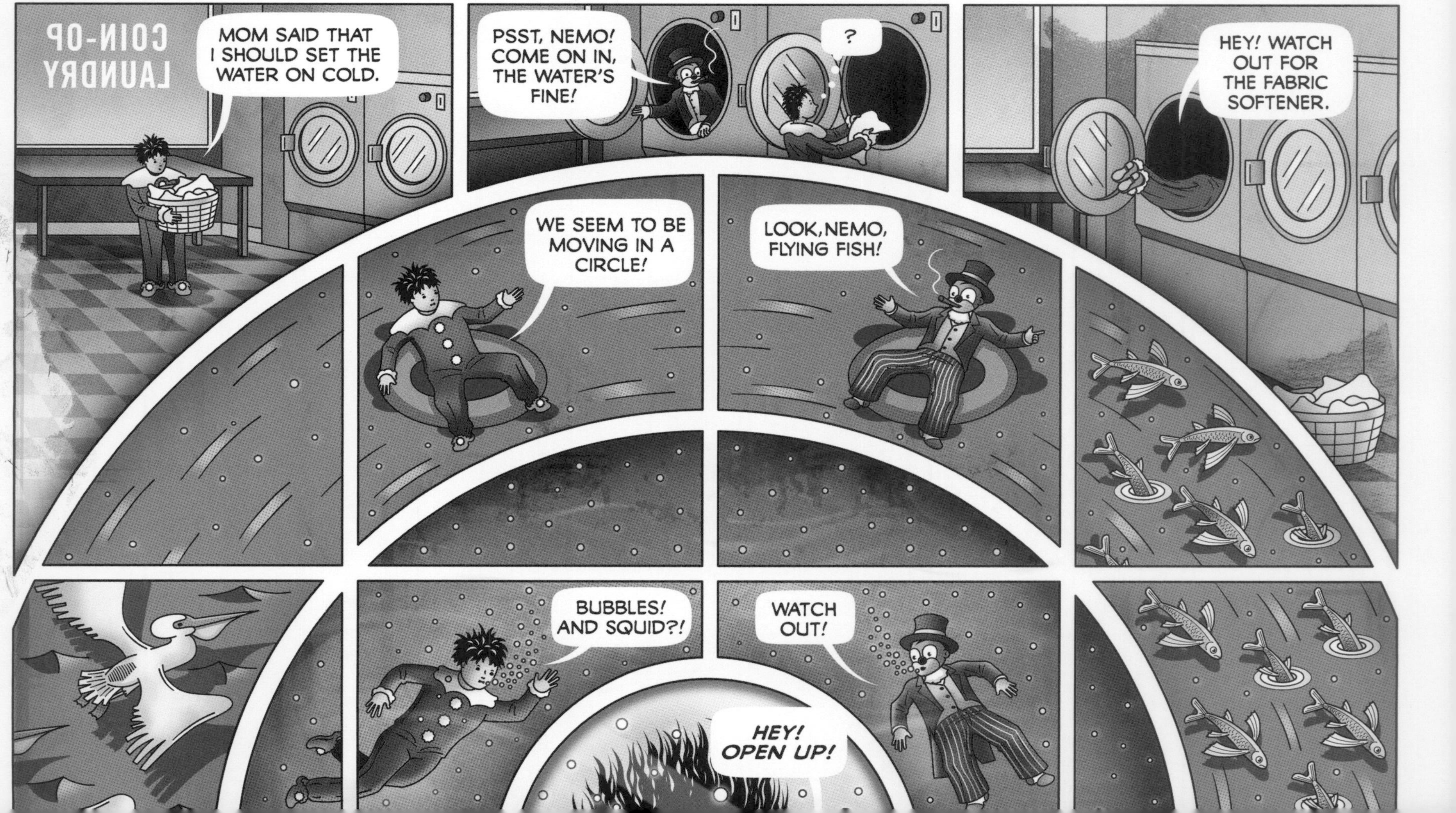
COIN-OP LAUNDRY
MOM SAID THAT I SHOULD SET THE WATER ON COLD.
PSST, NEMO! COME ON IN, THE WATER'S FINE!
?
HEY! WATCH OUT FOR THE FABRIC SOFTENER.
WE SEEM TO BE MOVING IN A CIRCLE!
LOOK, NEMO, FLYING FISH!
BUBBLES! AND SQUID?!
WATCH OUT!
HEY! OPEN UP!

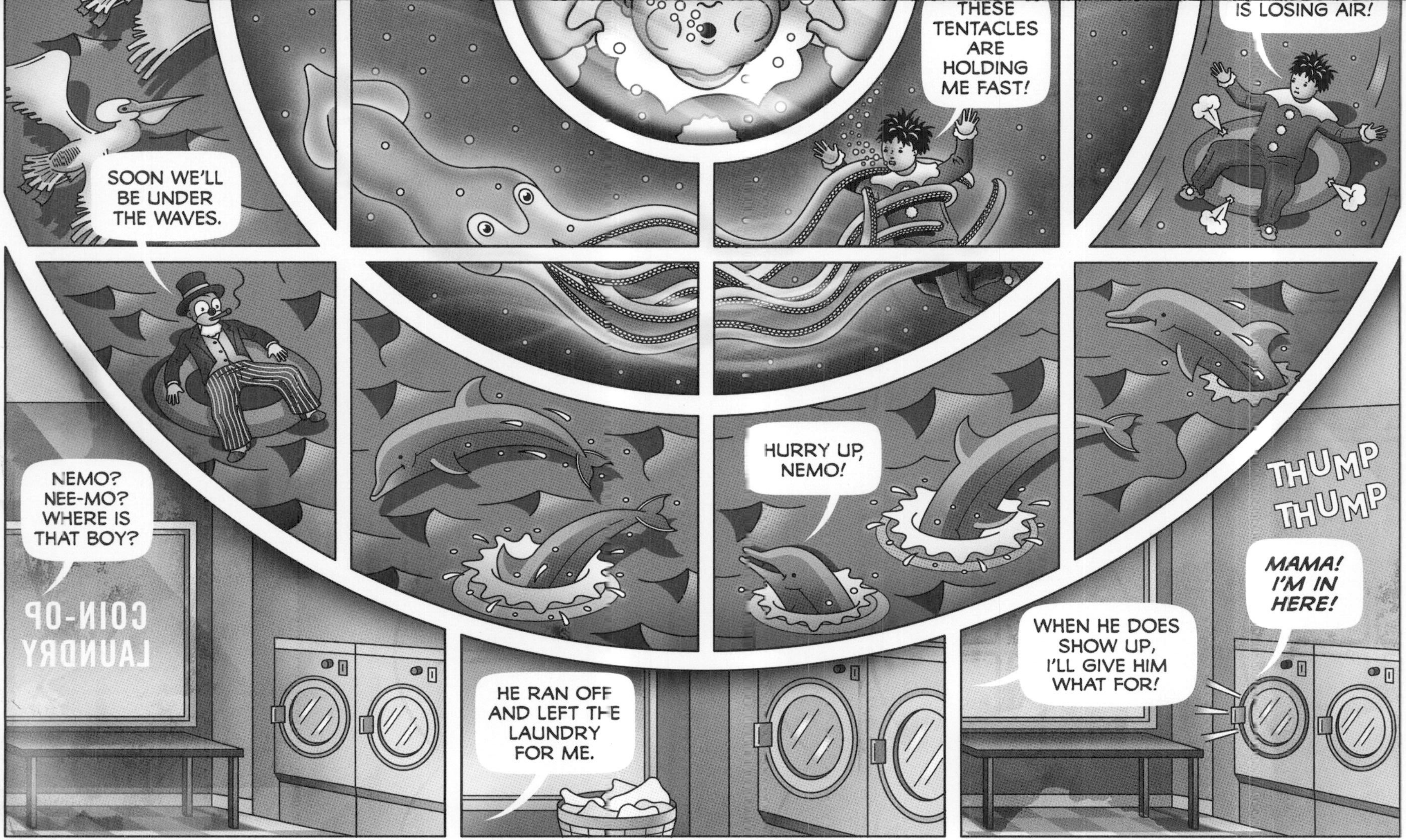
SOON WE'LL BE UNDER THE WAVES.
THESE TENTACLES ARE HOLDING ME FAST!
IS LOSING AIR!
NEMO? NEE-MO? WHERE IS THAT BOY?
COIN-OP LAUNDRY
HURRY UP, NEMO!
THUMP THUMP
MAMA! I'M IN HERE!
HE RAN OFF AND LEFT THE LAUNDRY FOR ME.
WHEN HE DOES SHOW UP, I'LL GIVE HIM WHAT FOR!

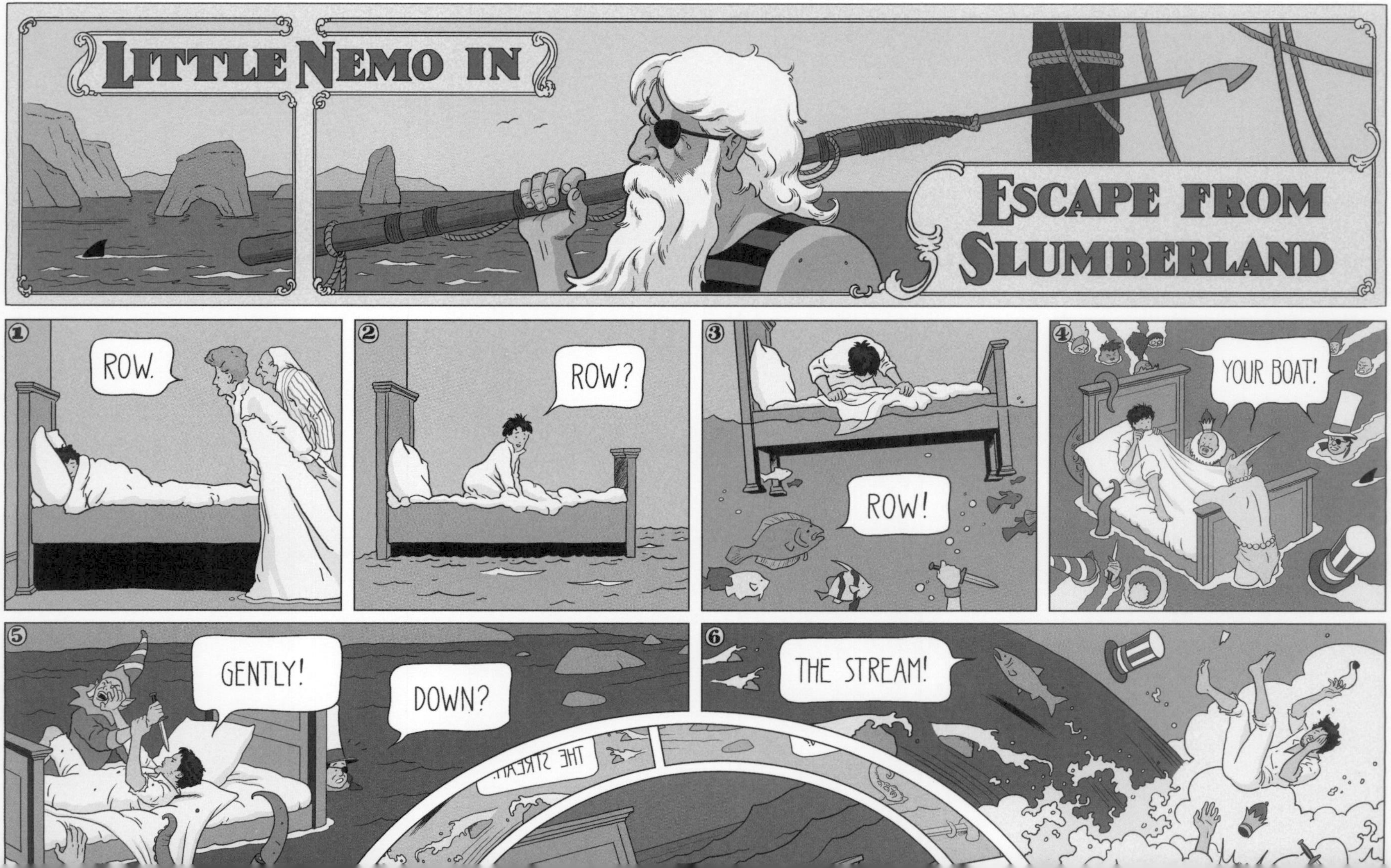
LITTLE NEMO IN
ESCAPE FROM SLUMBERLAND
ROW.
ROW?
ROW!
YOUR BOAT!
GENTLY!
DOWN?
THE STREAM!

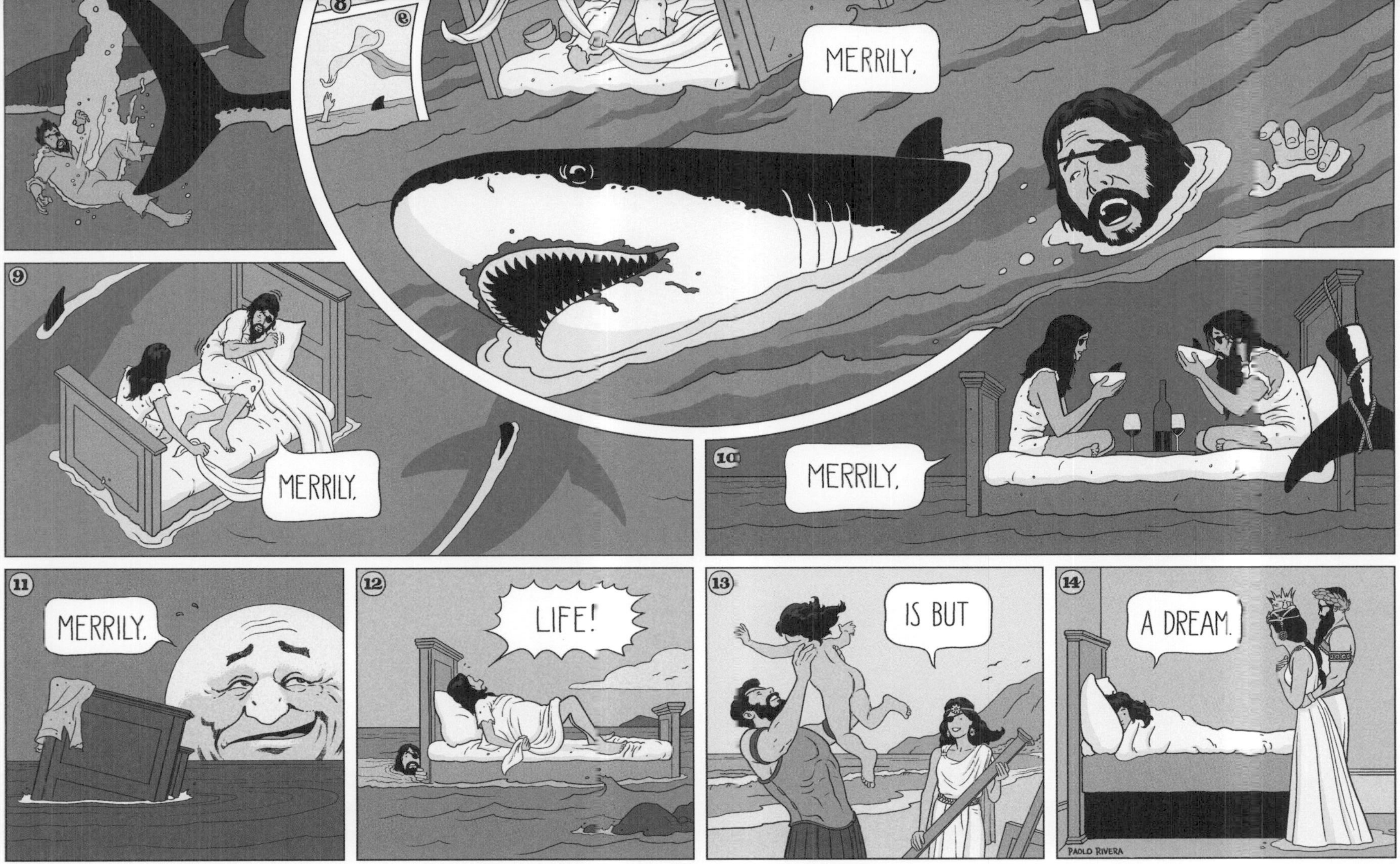
MERRILY,
MERRILY,
MERRILY,
MERRILY,
LIFE!
IS BUT
A DREAM.
PAOLO RIVERA

Paolo Rivera

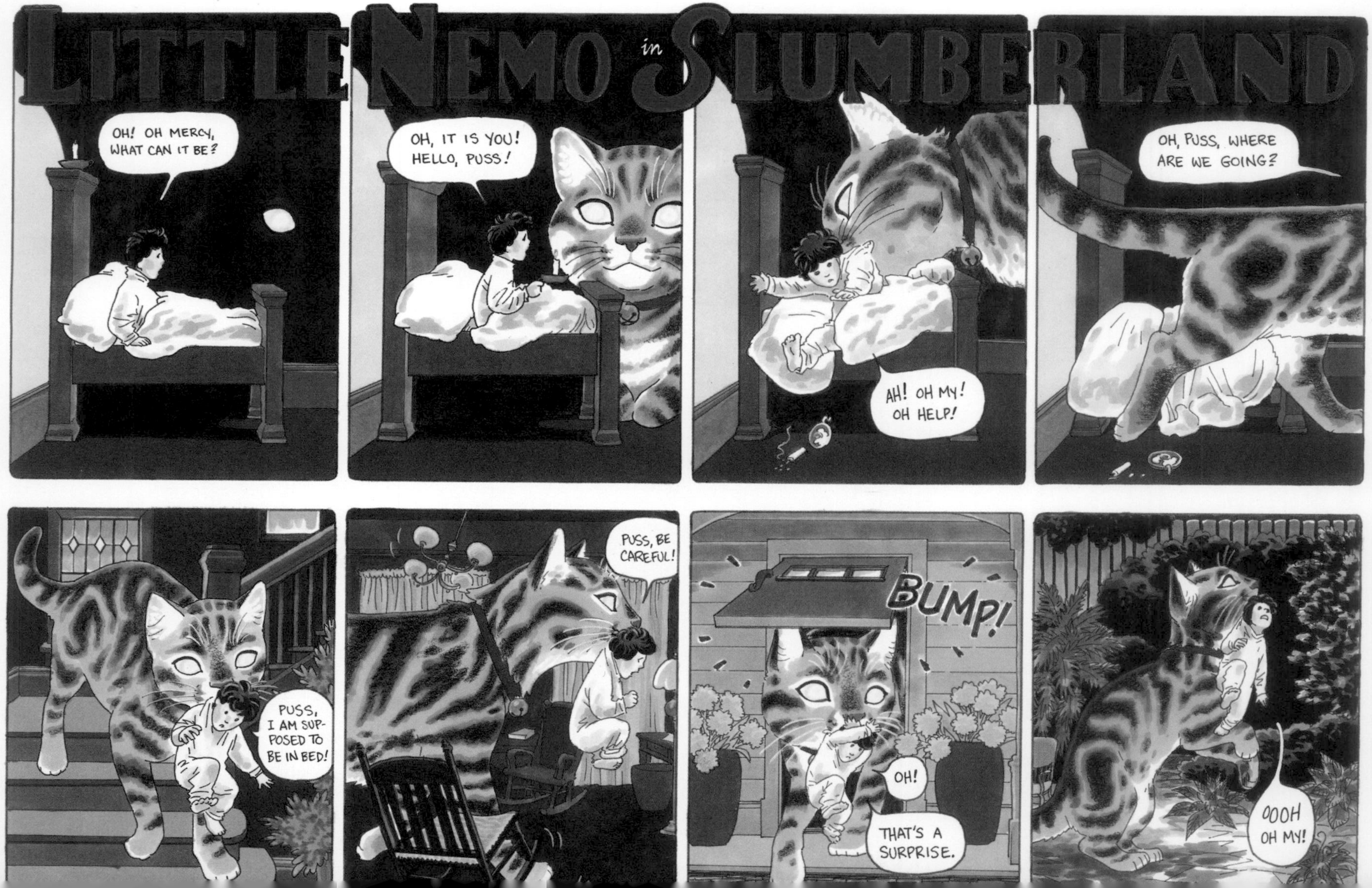
LITTLE NEMO in SLUMBERLAND
OH! OH MERCY, WHAT CAN IT BE?
OH, IT IS YOU! HELLO, PUSS!
AH! OH MY! OH HELP!
OH, PUSS, WHERE ARE WE GOING?
PUSS, I AM SUP-POSED TO BE IN BED!
PUSS, BE CAREFUL!
BUMP!
OH!
THAT'S A SURPRISE.
OOOH OH MY!

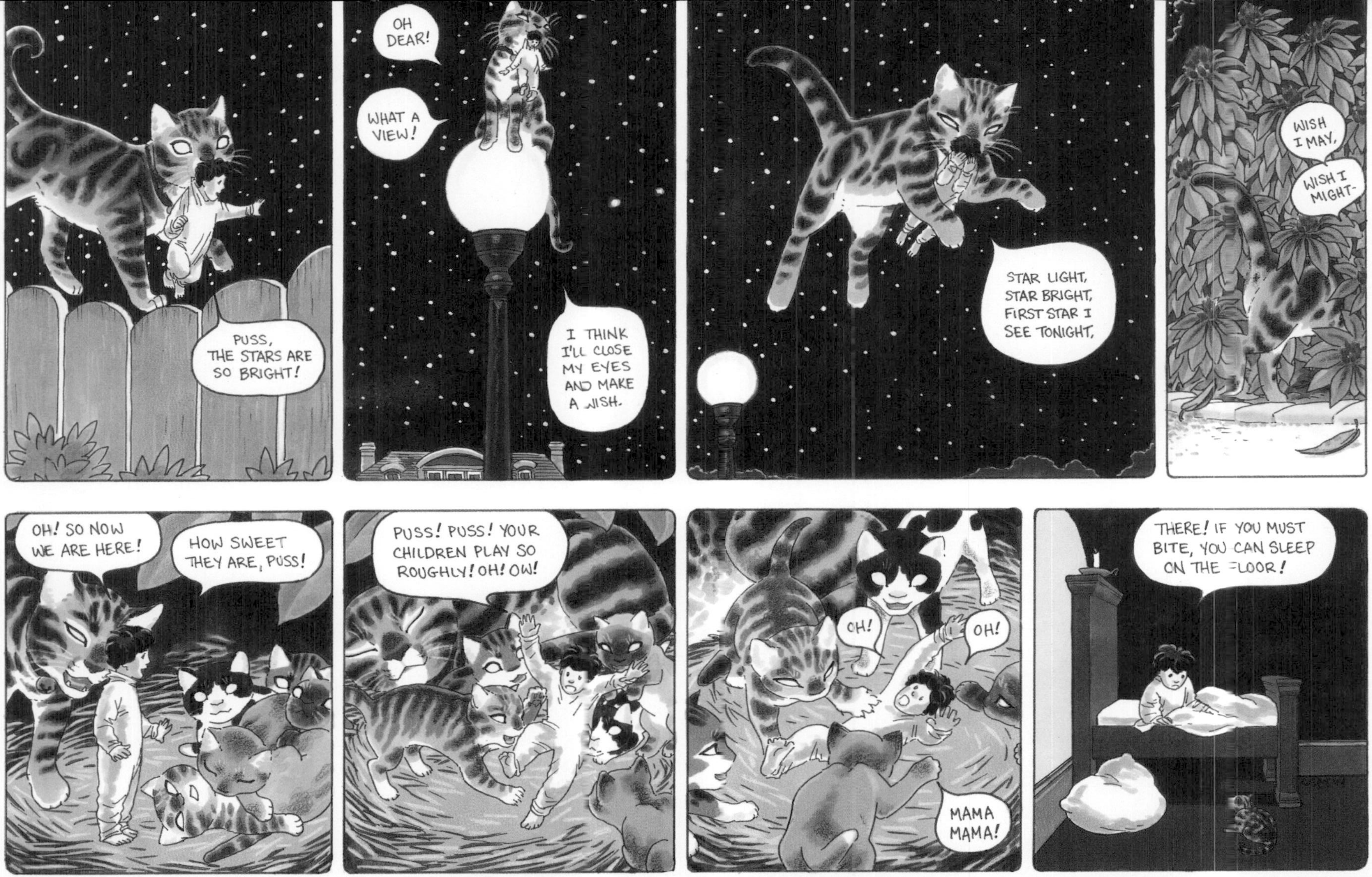
PUSS, THE STARS ARE SO BRIGHT!
OH DEAR!
WHAT A VIEW!
I THINK I'LL CLOSE MY EYES AND MAKE A WISH.
STAR LIGHT, STAR BRIGHT, FIRST STAR I SEE TONIGHT,
WISH I MAY,
WISH I MIGHT-
OH! SO NOW WE ARE HERE!
HOW SWEET THEY ARE, PUSS!
PUSS! PUSS! YOUR CHILDREN PLAY SO ROUGHLY! OH! OW!
OH!
OH!
MAMA MAMA!
THERE! IF YOU MUST BITE, YOU CAN SLEEP ON THE FLOOR!

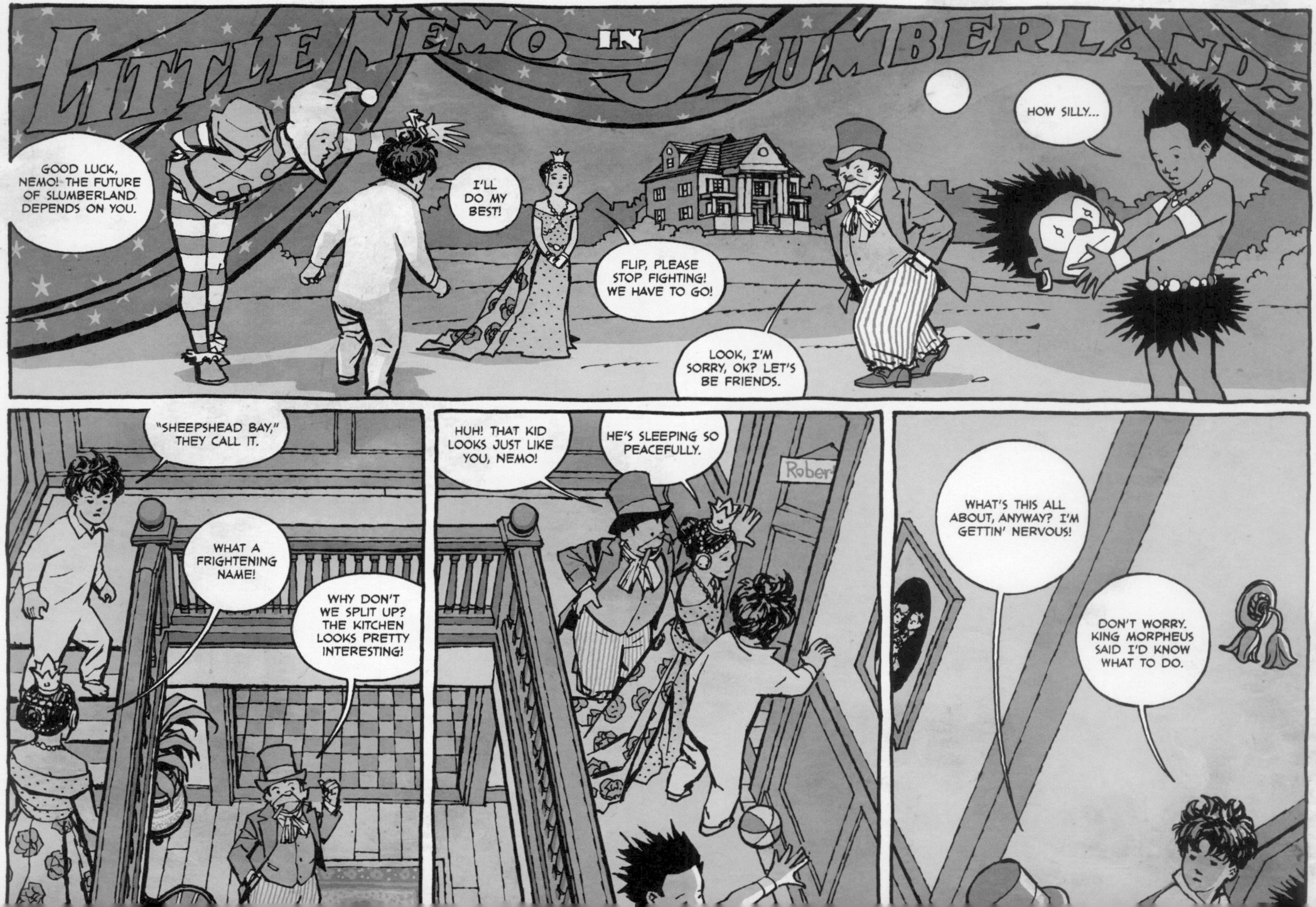
LITTLE NEMO IN SLUMBERLAND
GOOD LUCK, NEMO! THE FUTURE OF SLUMBERLAND DEPENDS ON YOU.
I'LL DO MY BEST!
FLIP, PLEASE STOP FIGHTING! WE HAVE TO GO!
LOOK, I'M SORRY, OK? LET'S BE FRIENDS.
HOW SILLY...
"SHEEPSHEAD BAY," THEY CALL IT.
WHAT A FRIGHTENING NAME!
WHY DON'T WE SPLIT UP? THE KITCHEN LOOKS PRETTY INTERESTING!
HUH! THAT KID LOOKS JUST LIKE YOU, NEMO!
HE'S SLEEPING SO PEACEFULLY.
Rober
WHAT'S THIS ALL ABOUT, ANYWAY? I'M GETTIN' NERVOUS!
DON'T WORRY. KING MORPHEUS SAID I'D KNOW WHAT TO DO.

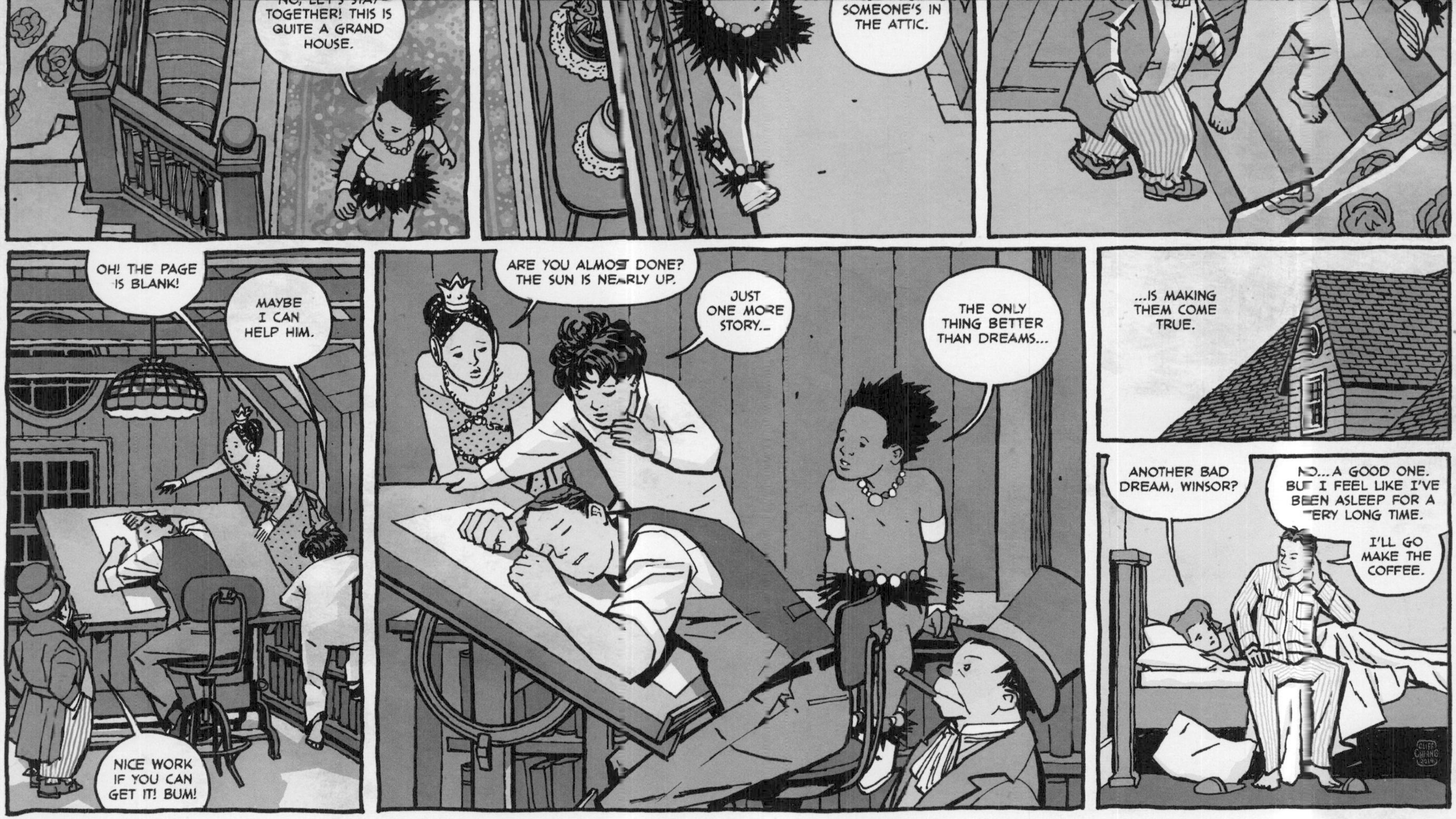
TOGETHER! THIS IS
QUITE A GRAND
HOUSE.
SOMEONE'S IN
THE ATTIC.
OH! THE PAGE
IS BLANK!
MAYBE
I CAN
HELP HIM.
NICE WORK
IF YOU CAN
GET IT! BUM!
ARE YOU ALMOST DONE?
THE SUN IS NEARLY UP.
JUST
ONE MORE
STORY...
THE ONLY
THING BETTER
THAN DREAMS...
...IS MAKING
THEM COME
TRUE.
ANOTHER BAD
DREAM, WINSOR?
NO... A GOOD ONE.
BUT I FEEL LIKE I'VE
BEEN ASLEEP FOR A
VERY LONG TIME.
I'LL GO
MAKE THE
COFFEE.
CLIFF CHIANG 2014

Cliff Chiang

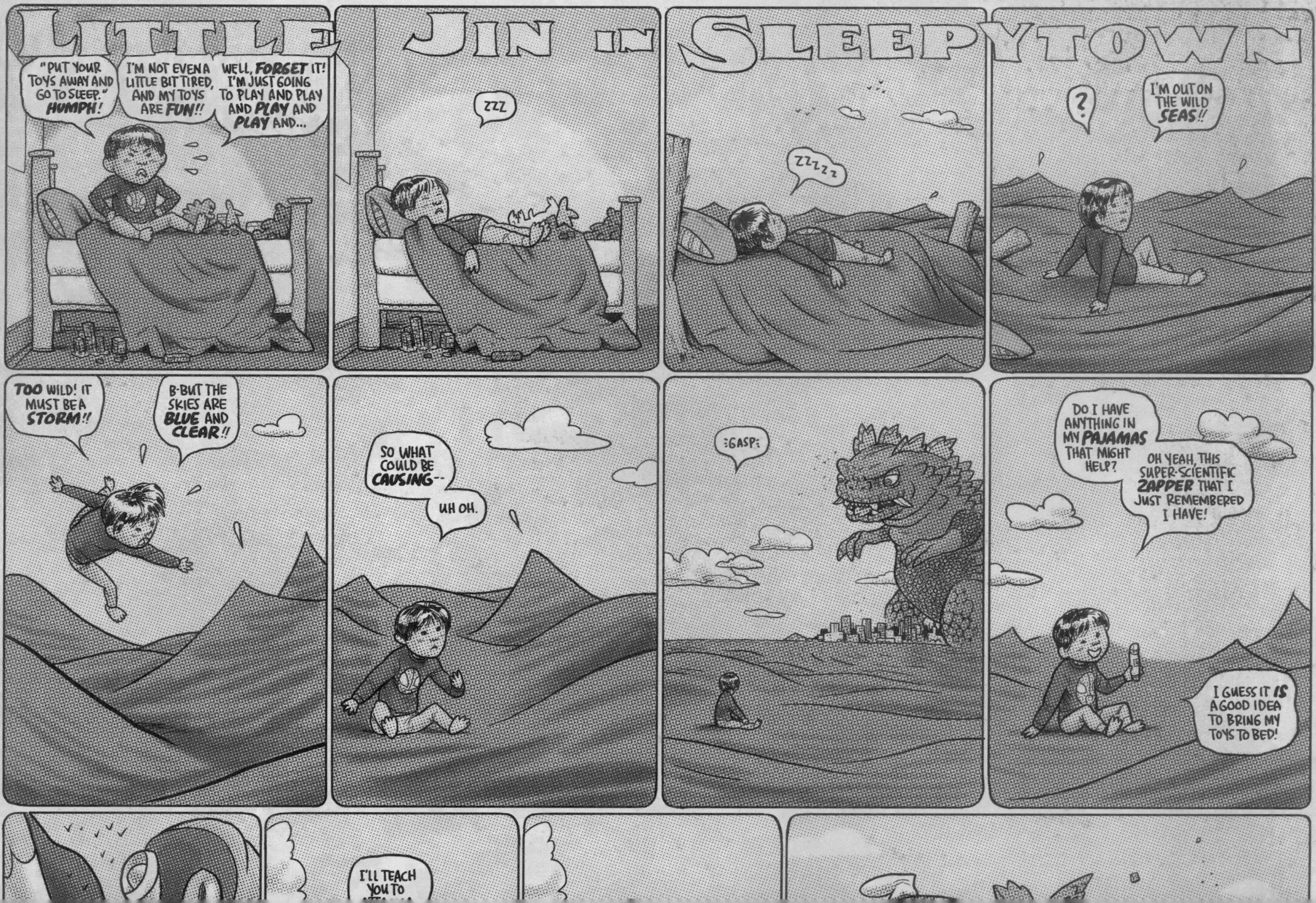
LITTLE JIN IN SLEEPYTOWN
"PUT YOUR TOYS AWAY AND GO TO SLEEP." HUMPH!
I'M NOT EVEN A LITTLE BIT TIRED, AND MY TOYS ARE FUN!!
WELL, FORGET IT! I'M JUST GOING TO PLAY AND PLAY AND PLAY AND PLAY AND...
ZZZ
ZZZZZ
?
I'M OUT ON THE WILD SEAS!!
TOO WILD! IT MUST BE A STORM!!
B-BUT THE SKIES ARE BLUE AND CLEAR!!
SO WHAT COULD BE CAUSING--
UH OH.
GASP
DO I HAVE ANYTHING IN MY PAJAMAS THAT MIGHT HELP?
OH YEAH, THIS SUPER-SCIENTIFIC ZAPPER THAT I JUST REMEMBERED I HAVE!
I GUESS IT IS A GOOD IDEA TO BRING MY TOYS TO BED!
I'LL TEACH YOU TO

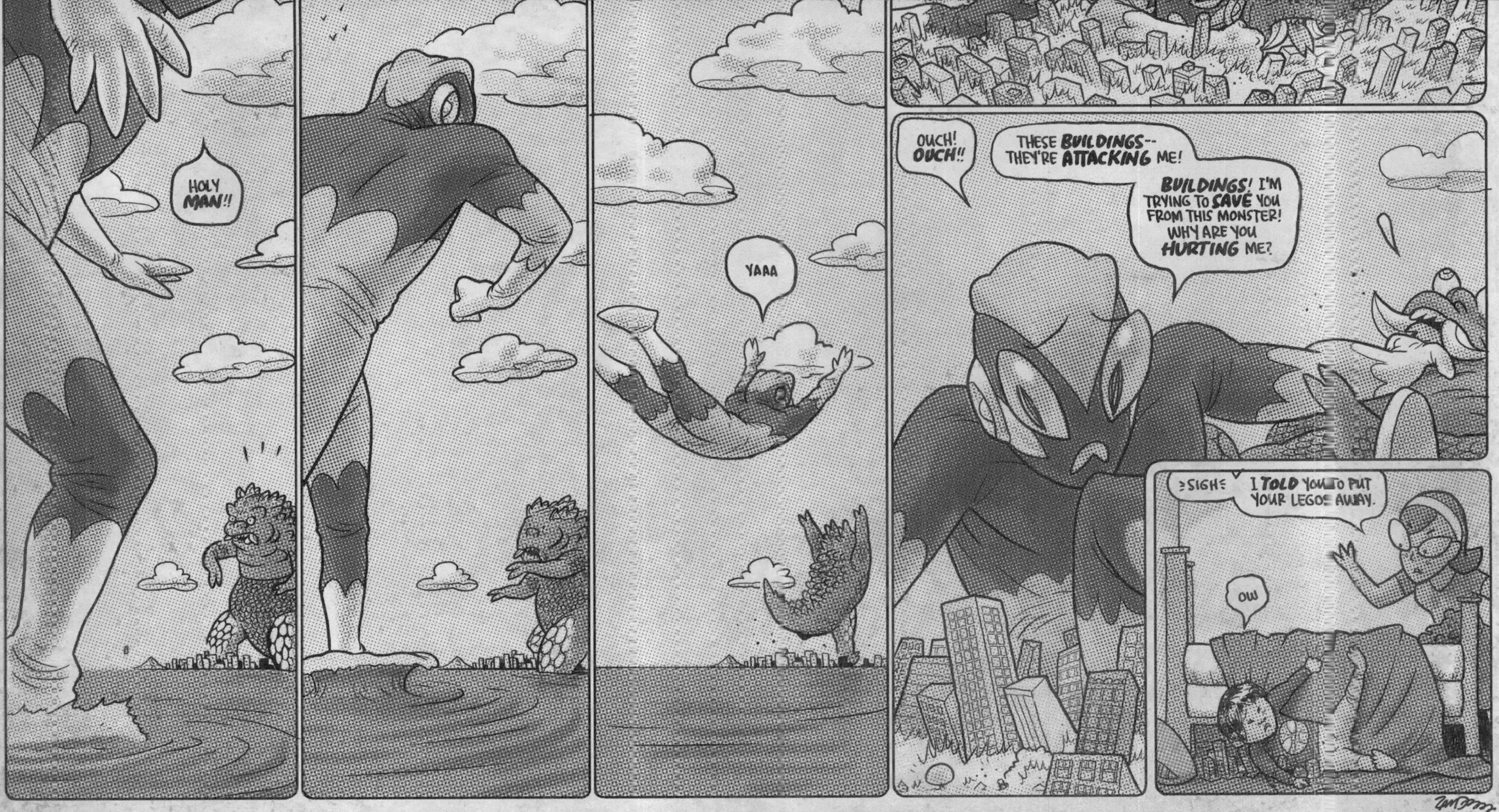
HOLY MAN!!
YAAA
OUCH! OUCH!!
THESE BUILDINGS-- THEY'RE ATTACKING ME!
BUILDINGS! I'M TRYING TO SAVE YOU FROM THIS MONSTER! WHY ARE YOU HURTING ME?
≡SIGH≡
I TOLD YOU TO PUT YOUR LEGOS AWAY.
OW

Zander Cannon

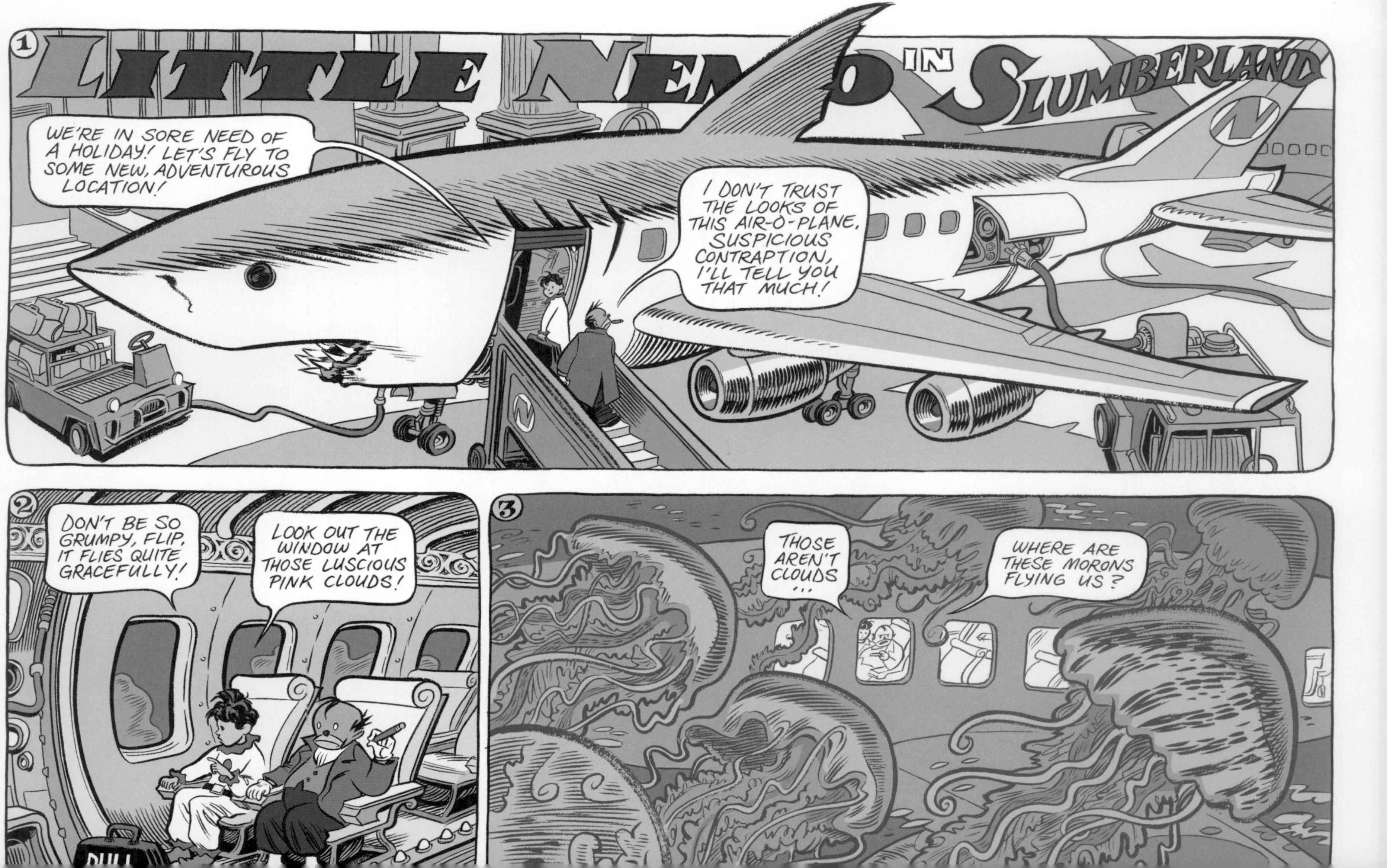
1
LITTLE NEMO IN SLUMBERLAND
WE'RE IN SORE NEED OF A HOLIDAY! LET'S FLY TO SOME NEW, ADVENTUROUS LOCATION!
I DON'T TRUST THE LOOKS OF THIS AIR-O-PLANE. SUSPICIOUS CONTRAPTION, I'LL TELL YOU THAT MUCH!
2
DON'T BE SO GRUMPY, FLIP, IT FLIES QUITE GRACEFULLY!
LOOK OUT THE WINDOW AT THOSE LUSCIOUS PINK CLOUDS!
3
THOSE AREN'T CLOUDS ...
WHERE ARE THESE MORONS FLYING US?

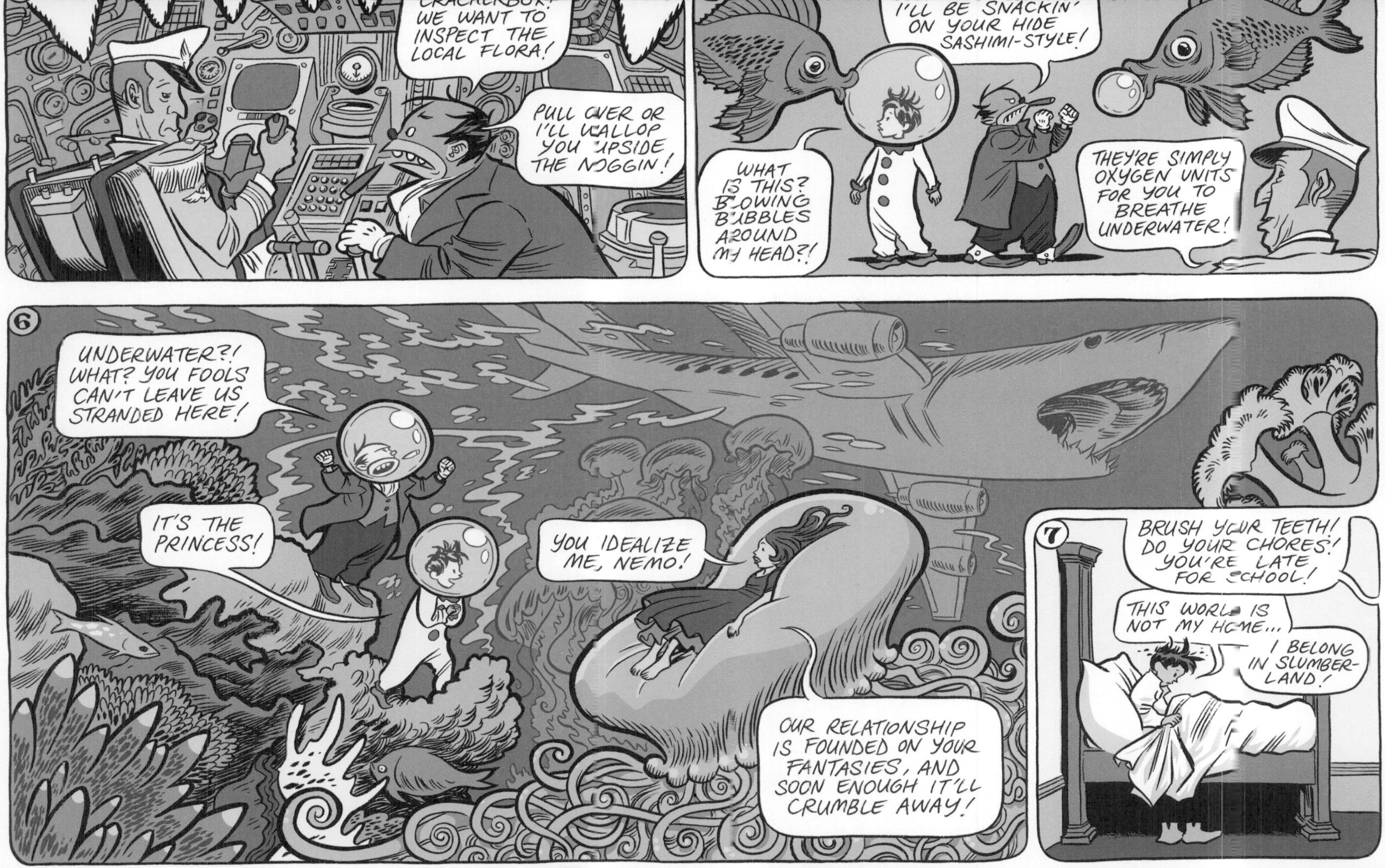
WE WANT TO INSPECT THE LOCAL FLORA!
PULL OVER OR I'LL WALLOP YOU UPSIDE THE NOGGIN!
I'LL BE SNACKIN' ON YOUR HIDE SASHIMI-STYLE!
WHAT IS THIS? BLOWING BUBBLES AROUND MY HEAD?!
THEY'RE SIMPLY OXYGEN UNITS FOR YOU TO BREATHE UNDERWATER!
6
UNDERWATER?! WHAT? YOU FOOLS CAN'T LEAVE US STRANDED HERE!
IT'S THE PRINCESS!
YOU IDEALIZE ME, NEMO!
OUR RELATIONSHIP IS FOUNDED ON YOUR FANTASIES, AND SOON ENOUGH IT'LL CRUMBLE AWAY!
7
BRUSH YOUR TEETH! DO YOUR CHORES! YOU'RE LATE FOR SCHOOL!
THIS WORLD IS NOT MY HOME...
I BELONG IN SLUMBERLAND!

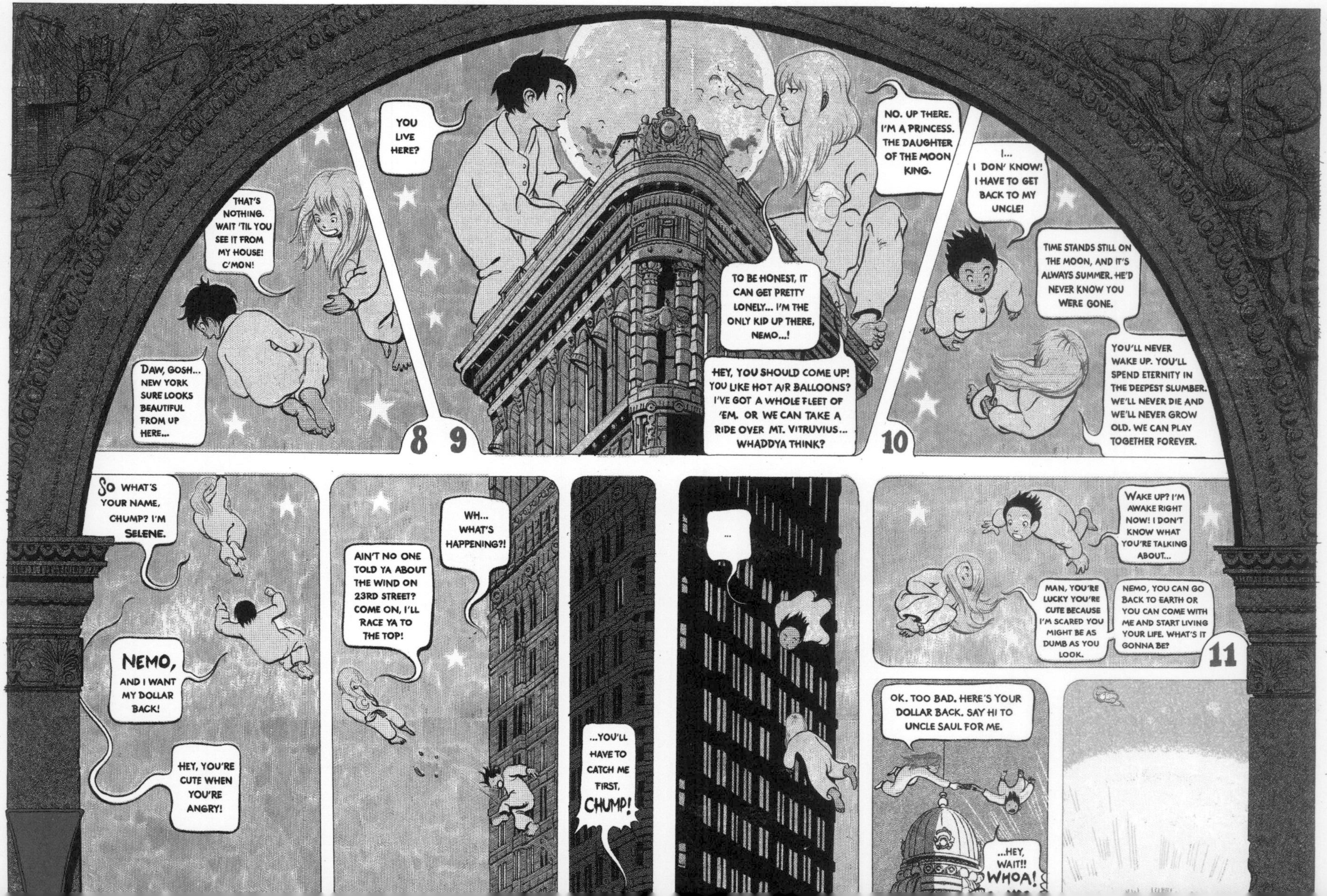
DAW, GOSH... NEW YORK SURE LOOKS BEAUTIFUL FROM UP HERE...
THAT'S NOTHING. WAIT 'TIL YOU SEE IT FROM MY HOUSE! C'MON!
8
YOU LIVE HERE?
9
NO. UP THERE. I'M A PRINCESS. THE DAUGHTER OF THE MOON KING.
TO BE HONEST, IT CAN GET PRETTY LONELY... I'M THE ONLY KID UP THERE, NEMO...!
HEY, YOU SHOULD COME UP! YOU LIKE HOT AIR BALLOONS? I'VE GOT A WHOLE FLEET OF 'EM. OR WE CAN TAKE A RIDE OVER MT. VITRUVIUS... WHADDYA THINK?
10
I... I DON' KNOW! I HAVE TO GET BACK TO MY UNCLE!
TIME STANDS STILL ON THE MOON, AND IT'S ALWAYS SUMMER. HE'D NEVER KNOW YOU WERE GONE.
YOU'LL NEVER WAKE UP. YOU'LL SPEND ETERNITY IN THE DEEPEST SLUMBER. WE'LL NEVER DIE AND WE'LL NEVER GROW OLD. WE CAN PLAY TOGETHER FOREVER.
SO WHAT'S YOUR NAME, CHUMP? I'M SELENE.
NEMO, AND I WANT MY DOLLAR BACK!
HEY, YOU'RE CUTE WHEN YOU'RE ANGRY!
AIN'T NO ONE TOLD YA ABOUT THE WIND ON 23RD STREET? COME ON, I'LL RACE YA TO THE TOP!
WH... WHAT'S HAPPENING?!
...YOU'LL HAVE TO CATCH ME FIRST, CHUMP!
...
WAKE UP? I'M AWAKE RIGHT NOW! I DON'T KNOW WHAT YOU'RE TALKING ABOUT...
MAN, YOU'RE LUCKY YOU'RE CUTE BECAUSE I'M SCARED YOU MIGHT BE AS DUMB AS YOU LOOK.
NEMO, YOU CAN GO BACK TO EARTH OR YOU CAN COME WITH ME AND START LIVING YOUR LIFE. WHAT'S IT GONNA BE?
11
OK. TOO BAD. HERE'S YOUR DOLLAR BACK. SAY HI TO UNCLE SAUL FOR ME.
...HEY, WAIT!! WHOA!

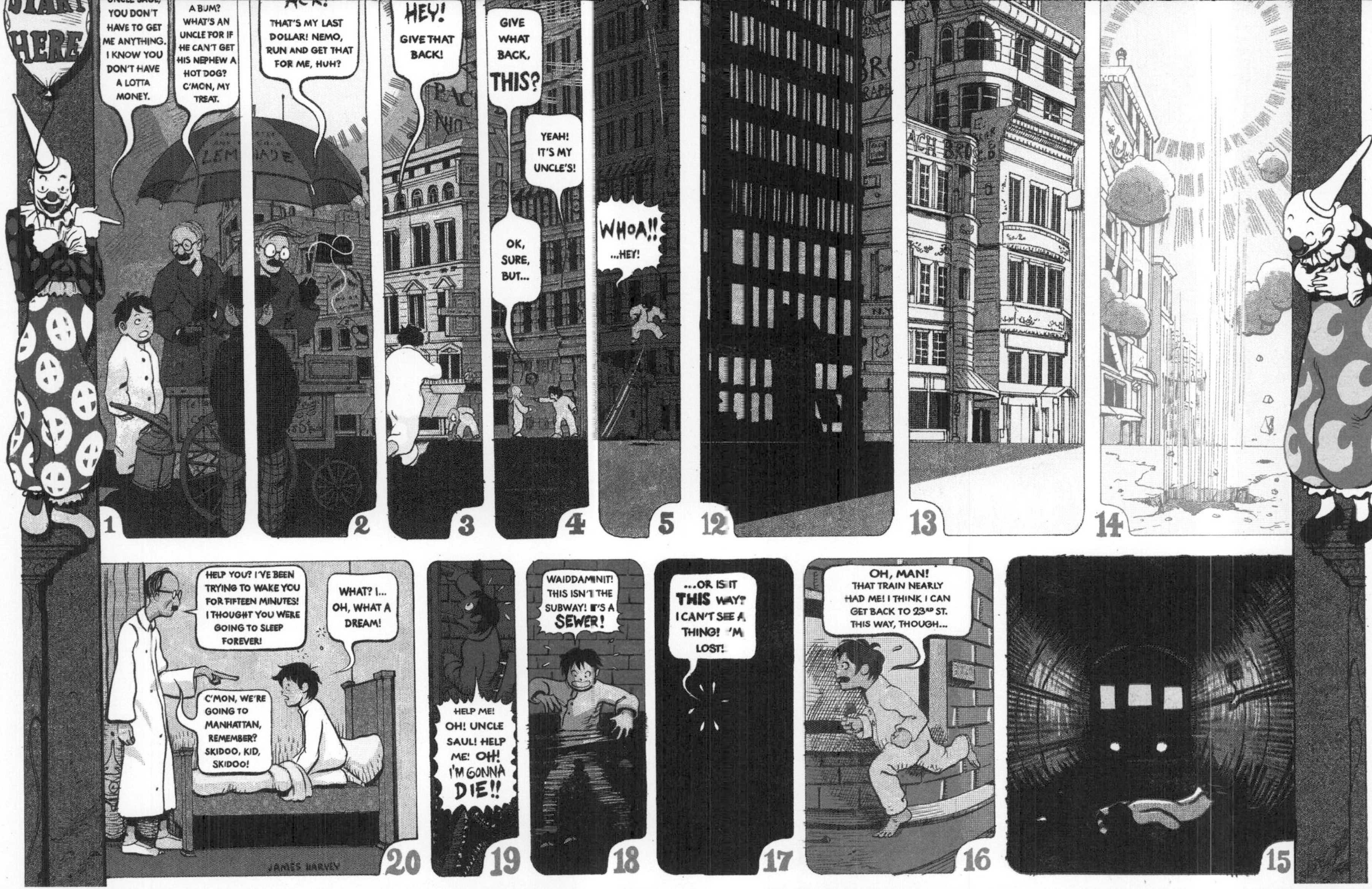
HERE
YOU DON'T HAVE TO GET ME ANYTHING. I KNOW YOU DON'T HAVE A LOTTA MONEY.
A BUM? WHAT'S AN UNCLE FOR IF HE CAN'T GET HIS NEPHEW A HOT DOG? C'MON, MY TREAT.
THAT'S MY LAST DOLLAR! NEMO, RUN AND GET THAT FOR ME, HUH?
HEY! GIVE THAT BACK!
GIVE WHAT BACK, THIS?
YEAH! IT'S MY UNCLE'S!
OK, SURE, BUT...
WHOA!! ...HEY!
OH, MAN! THAT TRAIN NEARLY HAD ME! I THINK I CAN GET BACK TO 23RD ST. THIS WAY, THOUGH...
...OR IS IT THIS WAY? I CAN'T SEE A THING! I'M LOST!
WAIDDAMINIT! THIS ISN'T THE SUBWAY! IT'S A SEWER!
HELP ME! OH! UNCLE SAUL! HELP ME! OH! I'M GONNA DIE!!
HELP YOU? I'VE BEEN TRYING TO WAKE YOU FOR FIFTEEN MINUTES! I THOUGHT YOU WERE GOING TO SLEEP FOREVER!
WHAT? I... OH, WHAT A DREAM!
C'MON, WE'RE GOING TO MANHATTAN, REMEMBER? SKIDOO, KID, SKIDOO!
JAMES HARVEY

James Harvey

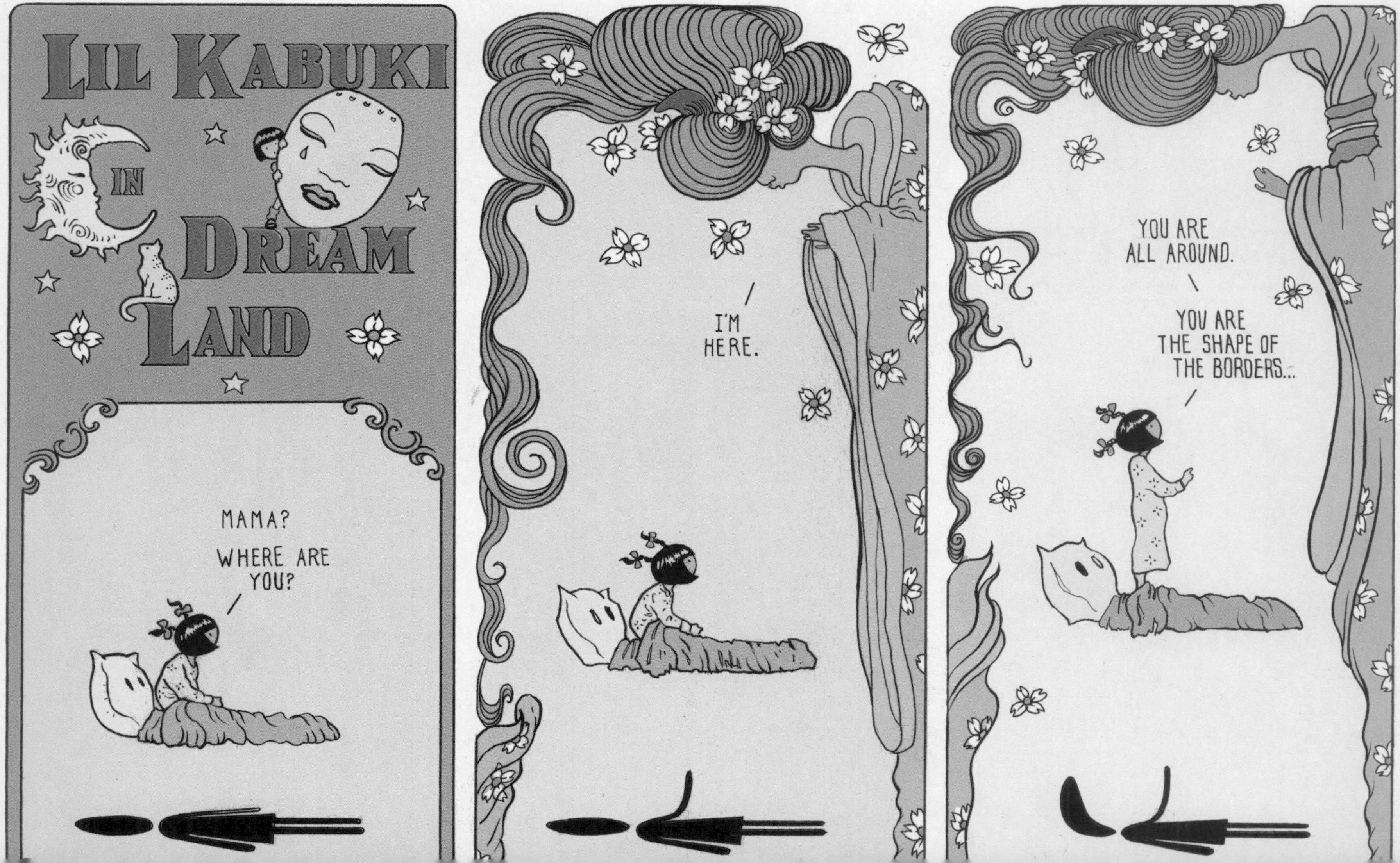
LIL KABUKI IN DREAM LAND
MAMA?
WHERE ARE YOU?
I'M HERE.
YOU ARE ALL AROUND.
YOU ARE THE SHAPE OF THE BORDERS...

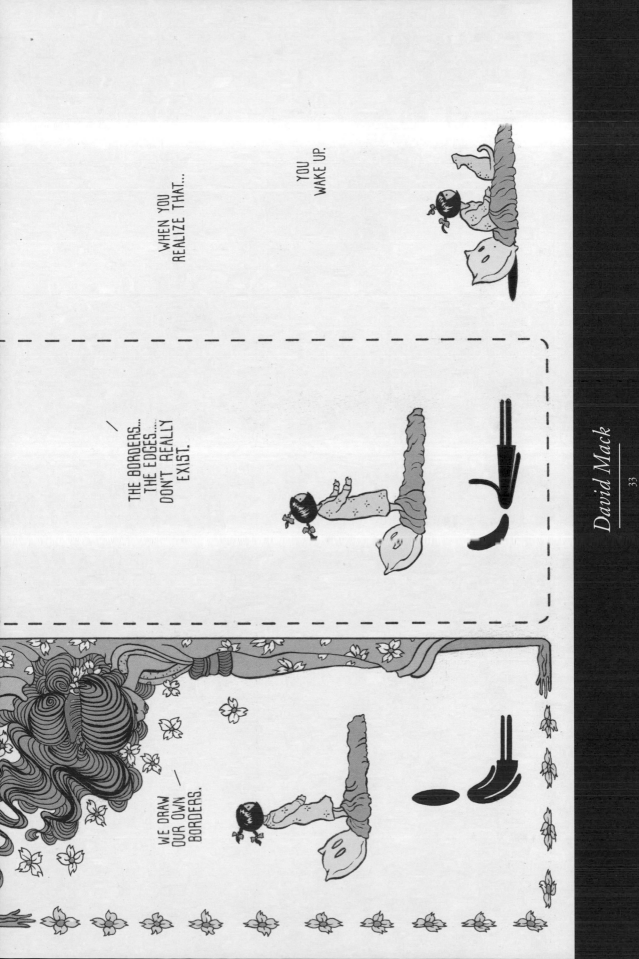

WHEN YOU
REALIZE THAT...

YOU
WAKE UP.

THE BORDERS...
THE EDGES....
DON'T REALLY
EXIST.

WE DRAW
OUR OWN
BORDERS.

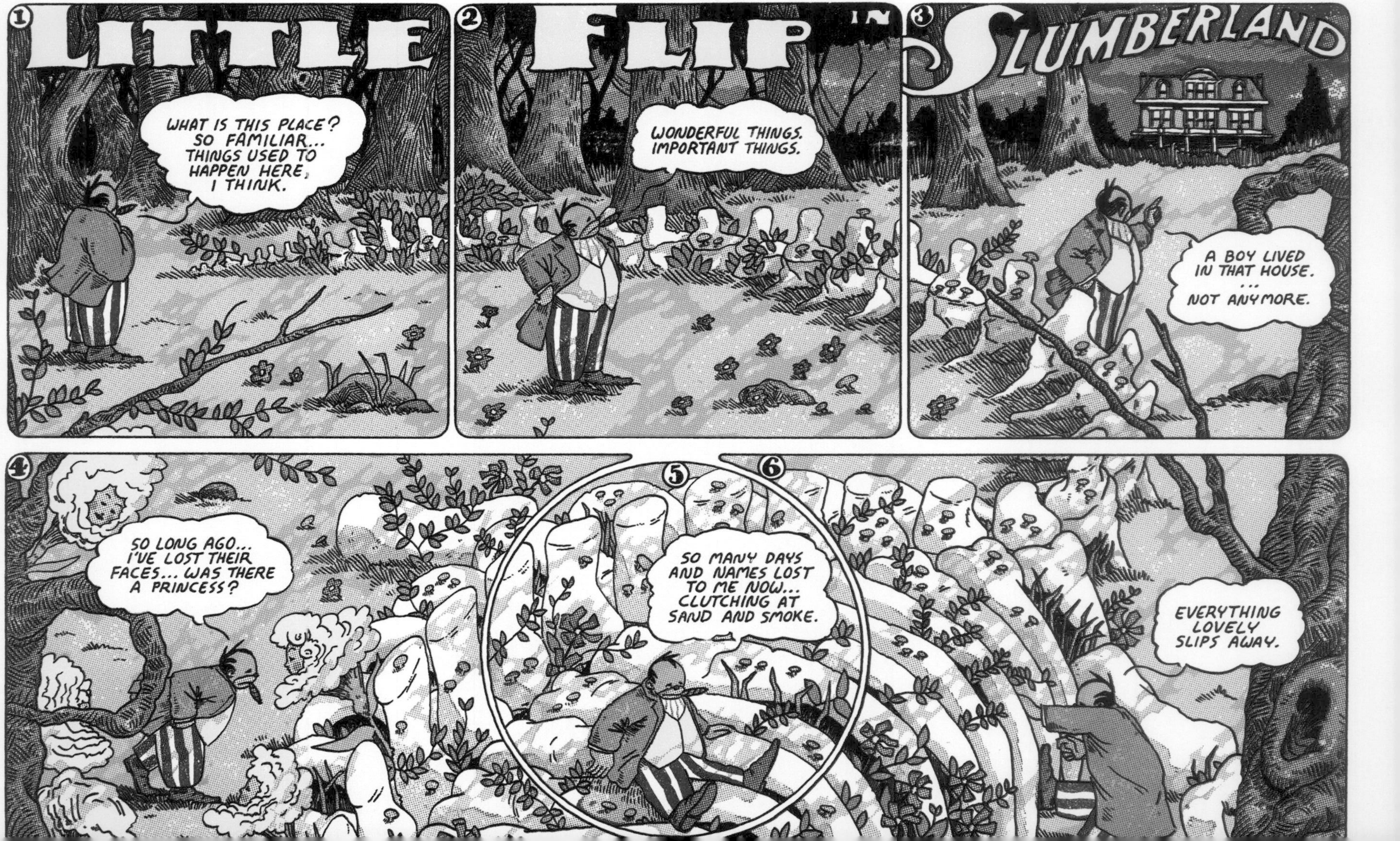
LITTLE FLIP IN SLUMBERLAND
WHAT IS THIS PLACE? SO FAMILIAR... THINGS USED TO HAPPEN HERE, I THINK.
WONDERFUL THINGS. IMPORTANT THINGS.
A BOY LIVED IN THAT HOUSE. ... NOT ANYMORE.
SO LONG AGO... I'VE LOST THEIR FACES... WAS THERE A PRINCESS?
SO MANY DAYS AND NAMES LOST TO ME NOW... CLUTCHING AT SAND AND SMOKE.
EVERYTHING LOVELY SLIPS AWAY.

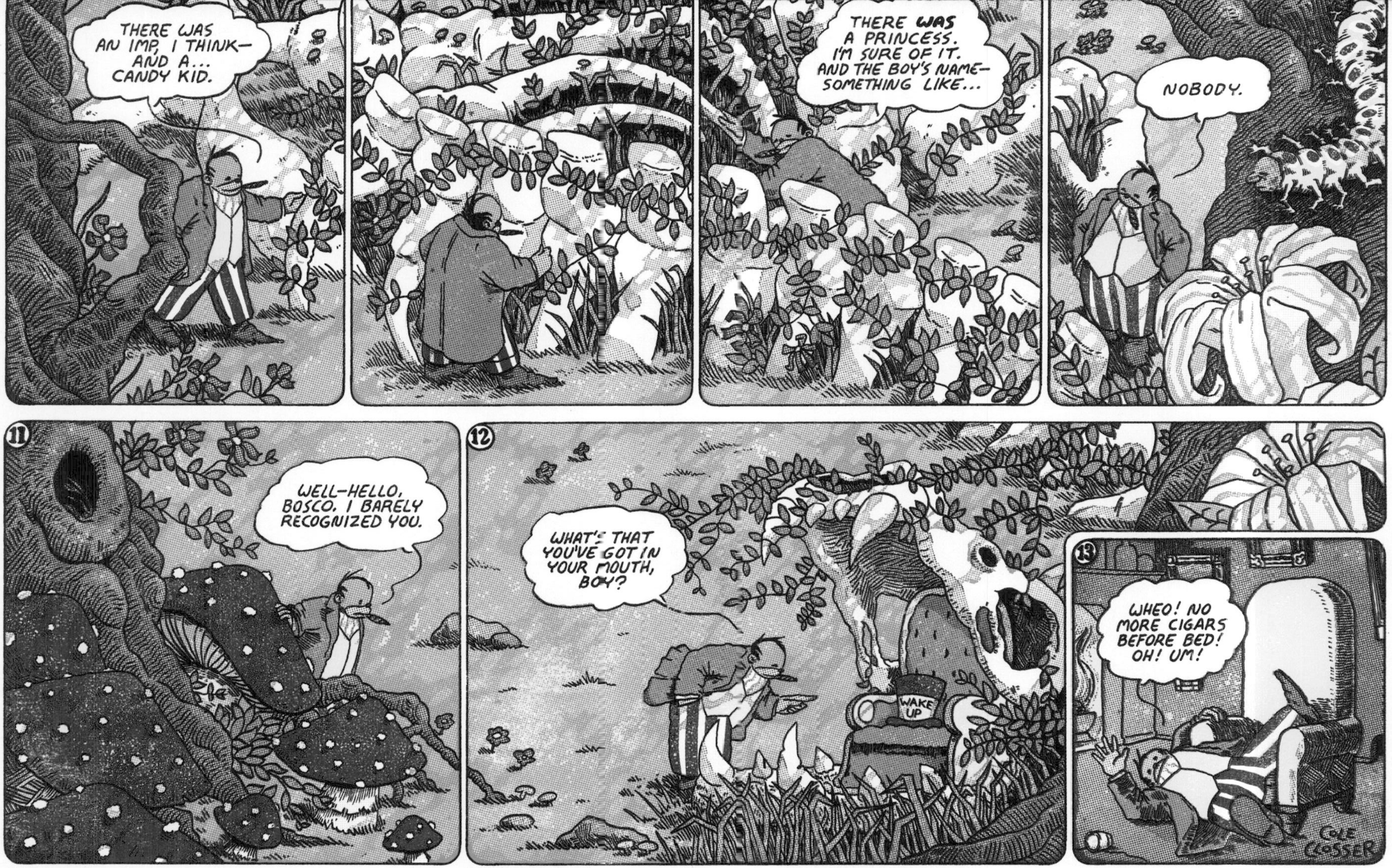
THERE WAS AN IMP, I THINK— AND A... CANDY KID.
THERE WAS A PRINCESS. I'M SURE OF IT. AND THE BOY'S NAME— SOMETHING LIKE...
NOBODY.
11
WELL—HELLO, BOSCO. I BARELY RECOGNIZED YOU.
12
WHAT'S THAT YOU'VE GOT IN YOUR MOUTH, BOY?
WAKE UP
13
WHEO! NO MORE CIGARS BEFORE BED! OH! UM!
COLE CLOSSER

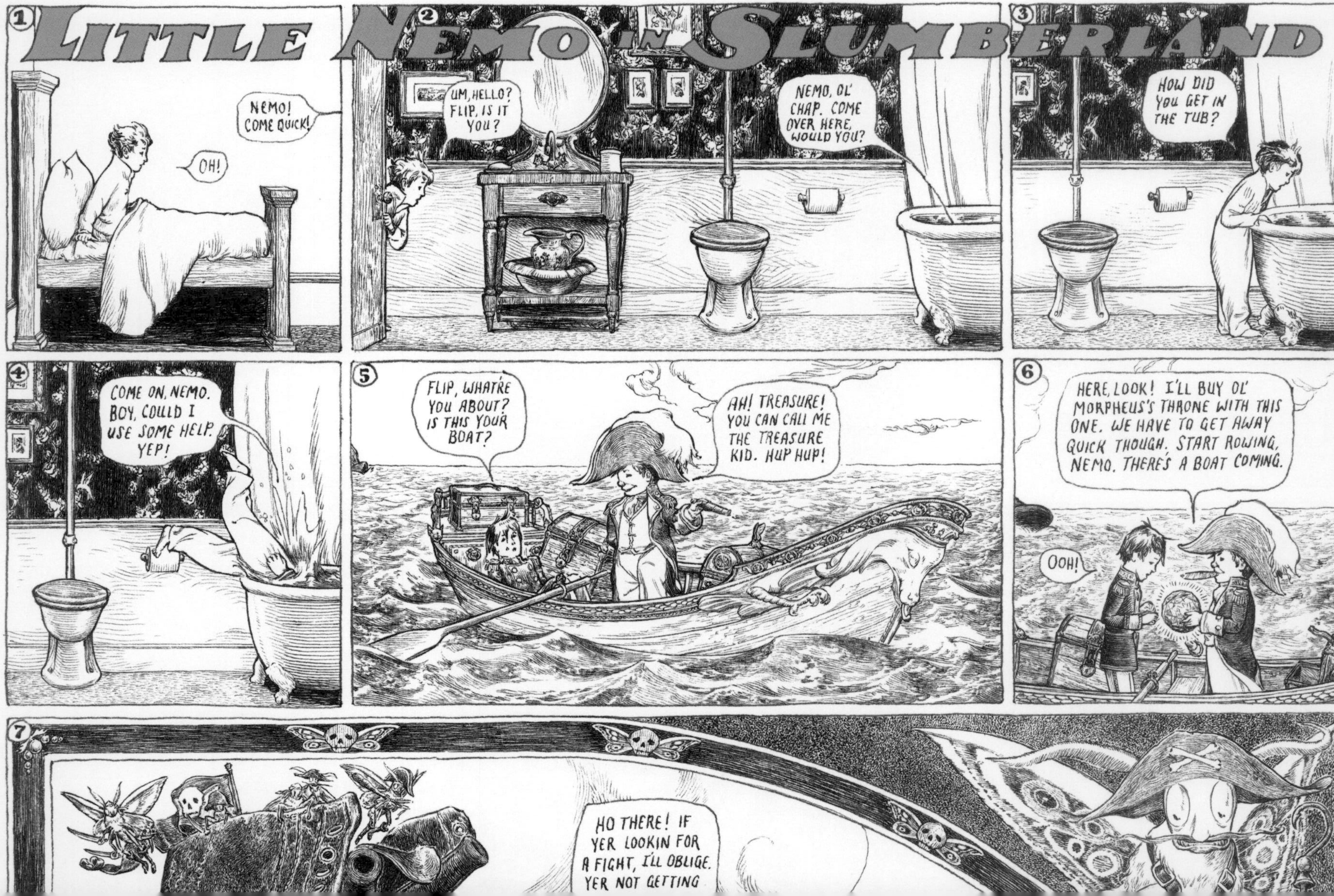
LITTLE NEMO IN SLUMBERLAND
1
NEMO! COME QUICK!
OH!
2
UM, HELLO? FLIP, IS IT YOU?
NEMO, OL' CHAP. COME OVER HERE, WOULD YOU?
3
HOW DID YOU GET IN THE TUB?
4
COME ON, NEMO. BOY, COULD I USE SOME HELP. YEP!
5
FLIP, WHAT'RE YOU ABOUT? IS THIS YOUR BOAT?
AH! TREASURE! YOU CAN CALL ME THE TREASURE KID. HUP HUP!
6
HERE, LOOK! I'LL BUY OL' MORPHEUS'S THRONE WITH THIS ONE. WE HAVE TO GET AWAY QUICK THOUGH. START ROWING, NEMO. THERE'S A BOAT COMING.
OOH!
7
HO THERE! IF YER LOOKIN FOR A FIGHT, I'LL OBLIGE. YER NOT GETTING

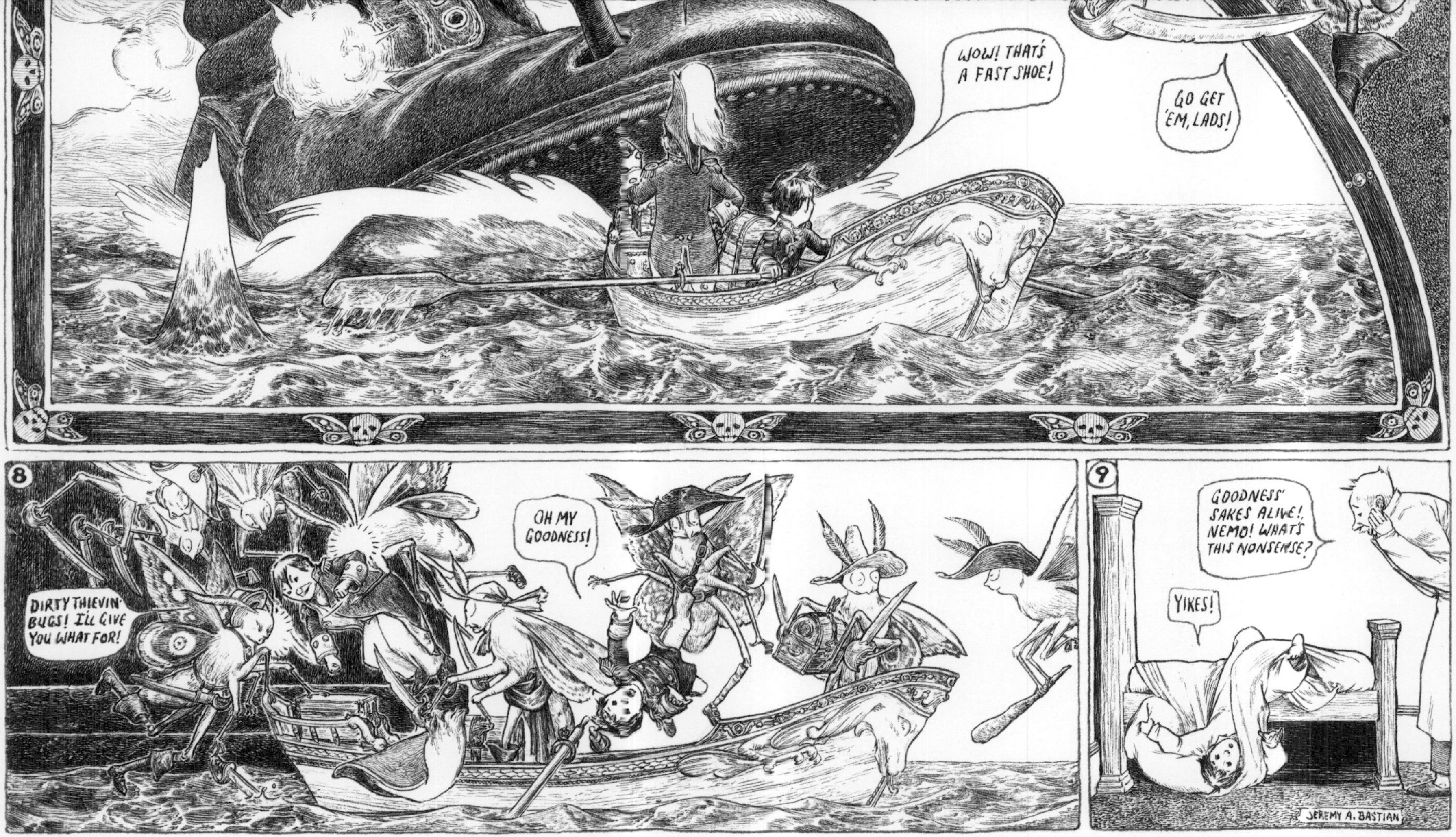
WOW! THAT'S A FAST SHOE!
GO GET 'EM, LADS!
8
DIRTY THIEVIN' BUGS! I'LL GIVE YOU WHAT FOR!
OH MY GOODNESS!
9
GOODNESS' SAKES ALIVE!, NEMO! WHAT'S THIS NONSENSE?
YIKES!
JEREMY A. BASTIAN

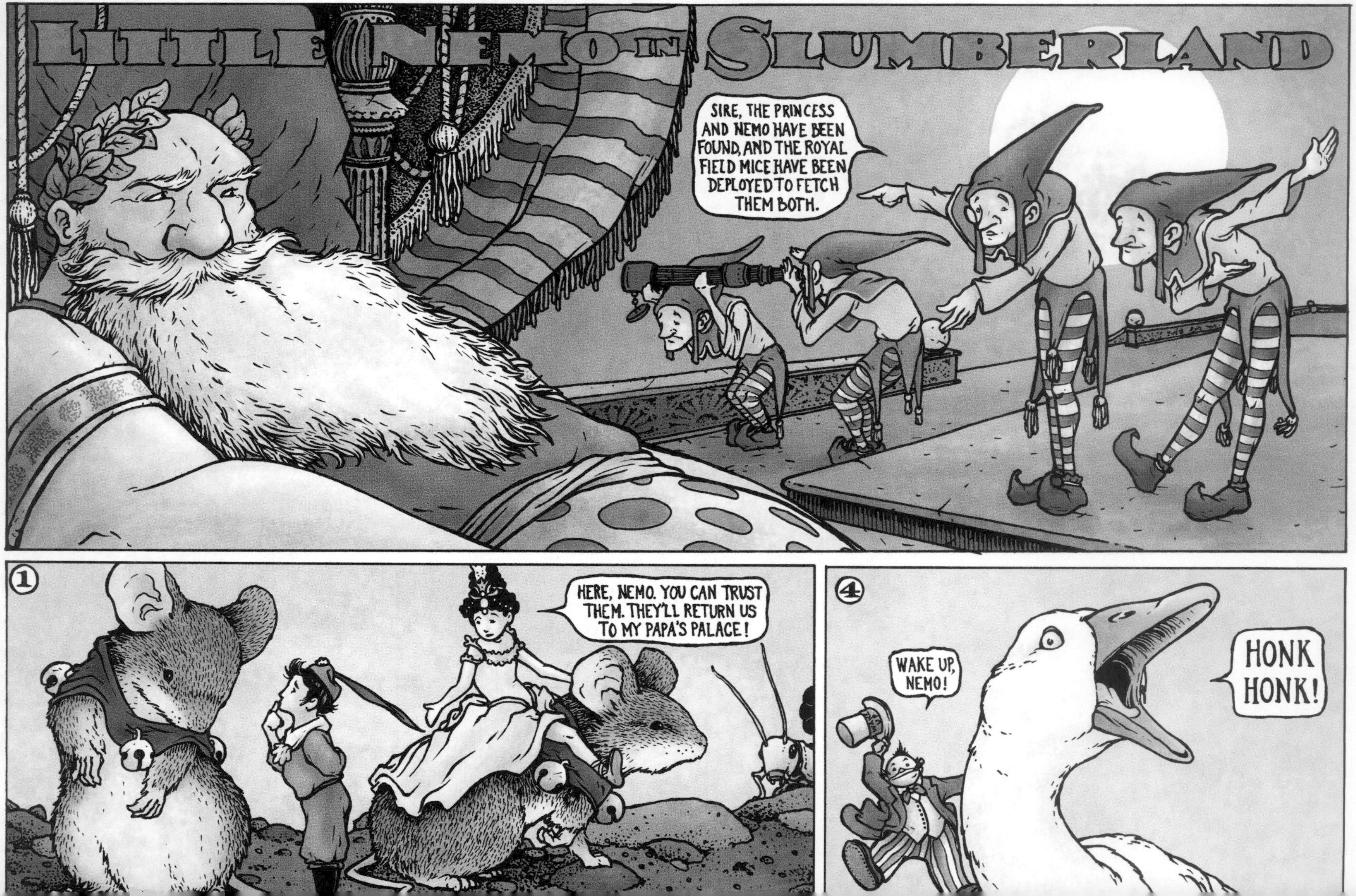
LITTLE NEMO IN SLUMBERLAND
SIRE, THE PRINCESS AND NEMO HAVE BEEN FOUND, AND THE ROYAL FIELD MICE HAVE BEEN DEPLOYED TO FETCH THEM BOTH.
1
HERE, NEMO. YOU CAN TRUST THEM. THEY'LL RETURN US TO MY PAPA'S PALACE!
4
WAKE UP, NEMO!
HONK HONK!

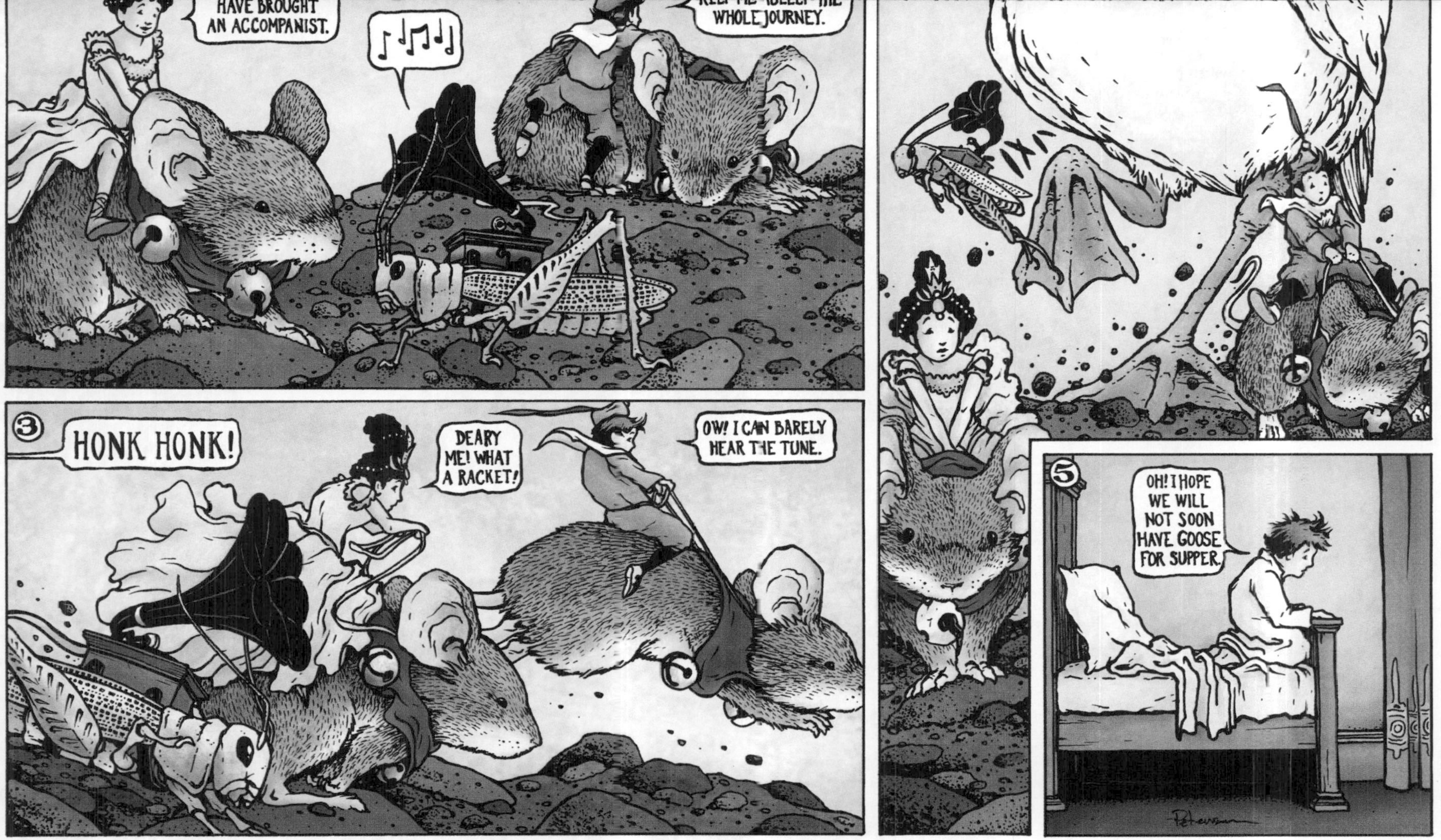
HAVE BROUGHT AN ACCOMPANIST.
WHOLE JOURNEY.
3
HONK HONK!
DEARY ME! WHAT A RACKET!
OW! I CAN BARELY HEAR THE TUNE.
5
OH! I HOPE WE WILL NOT SOON HAVE GOOSE FOR SUPPER.

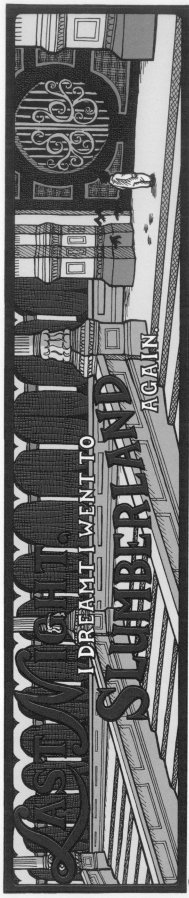

Last Night, I Dreamt I Went to Slumberland Again.

① IT SEEMED TO ME I STOOD BEFORE THE GATE, AND FOR A WHILE I COULD NOT ENTER, FOR THE WAY WAS BARRED TO ME...

② THEN, LIKE ALL DREAMERS, I WAS POSSESSED OF A SUDDEN WITH SUPERNATURAL POWERS

③ AND PASSED LIKE A SPIRIT THROUGH THE BARRIER BEFORE ME.

④ THE PATH WOUND AWAY BELOW ME, TWISTING AND TURNING AS IT ALWAYS HAD.

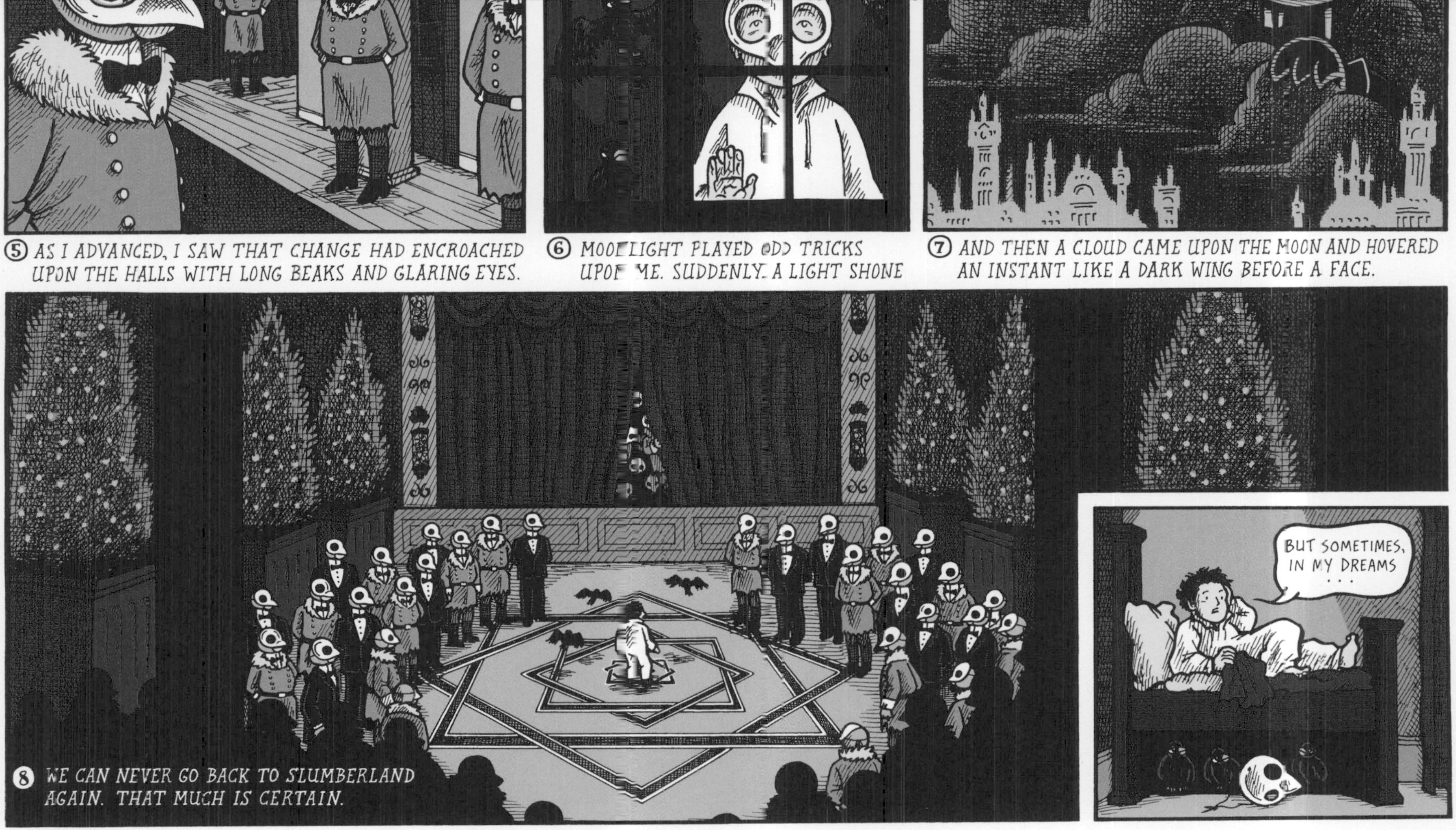
⑤ AS I ADVANCED, I SAW THAT CHANGE HAD ENCROACHED UPON THE HALLS WITH LONG BEAKS AND GLARING EYES.
⑥ MOONLIGHT PLAYED ODD TRICKS UPON ME. SUDDENLY, A LIGHT SHONE
⑦ AND THEN A CLOUD CAME UPON THE MOON AND HOVERED AN INSTANT LIKE A DARK WING BEFORE A FACE.
⑧ WE CAN NEVER GO BACK TO SLUMBERLAND AGAIN. THAT MUCH IS CERTAIN.
BUT SOMETIMES, IN MY DREAMS . . .

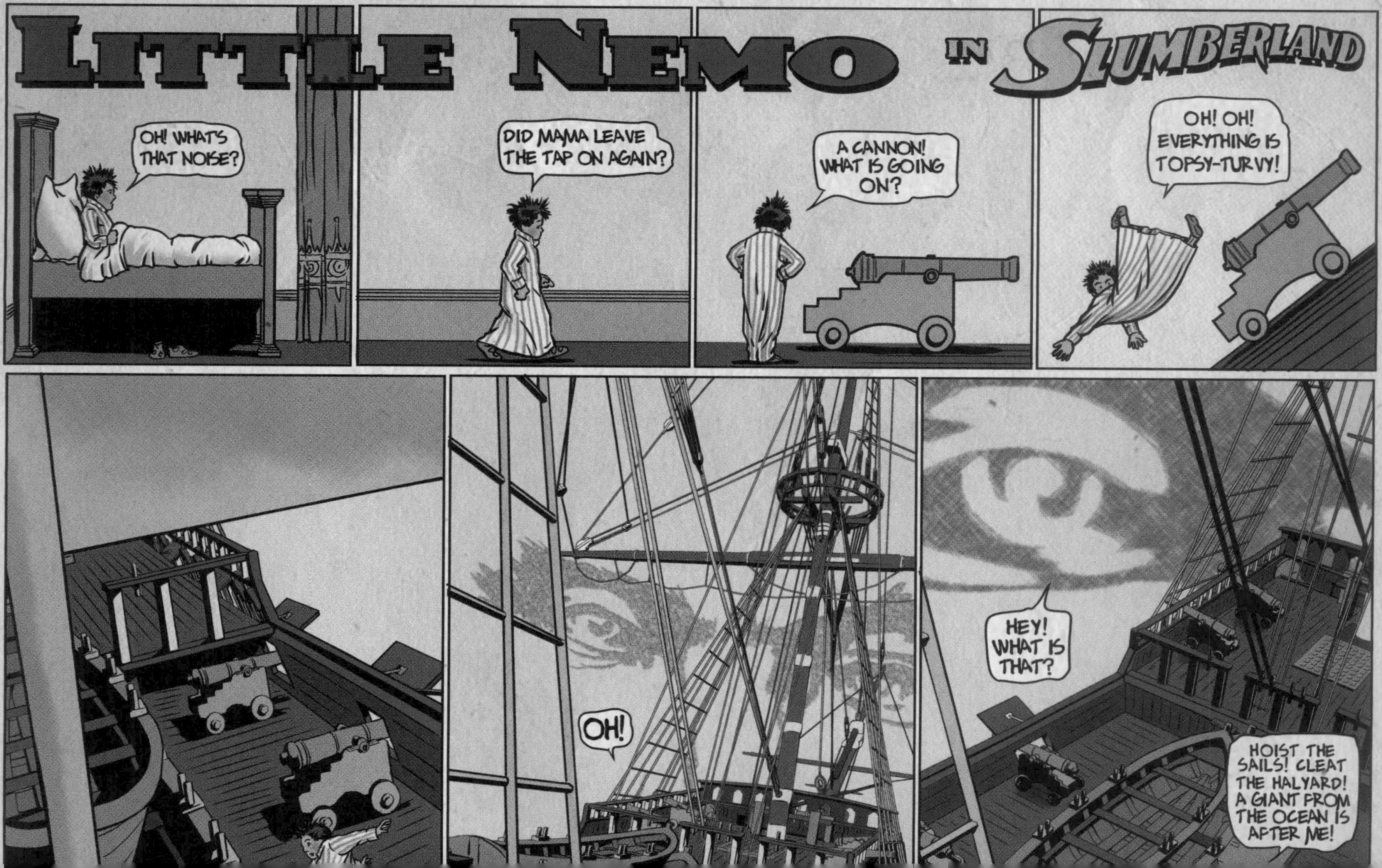
LITTLE NEMO IN SLUMBERLAND
OH! WHAT'S THAT NOISE?
DID MAMA LEAVE THE TAP ON AGAIN?
A CANNON! WHAT IS GOING ON?
OH! OH! EVERYTHING IS TOPSY-TURVY!
OH!
HEY! WHAT IS THAT?
HOIST THE SAILS! CLEAT THE HALYARD! A GIANT FROM THE OCEAN IS AFTER ME!

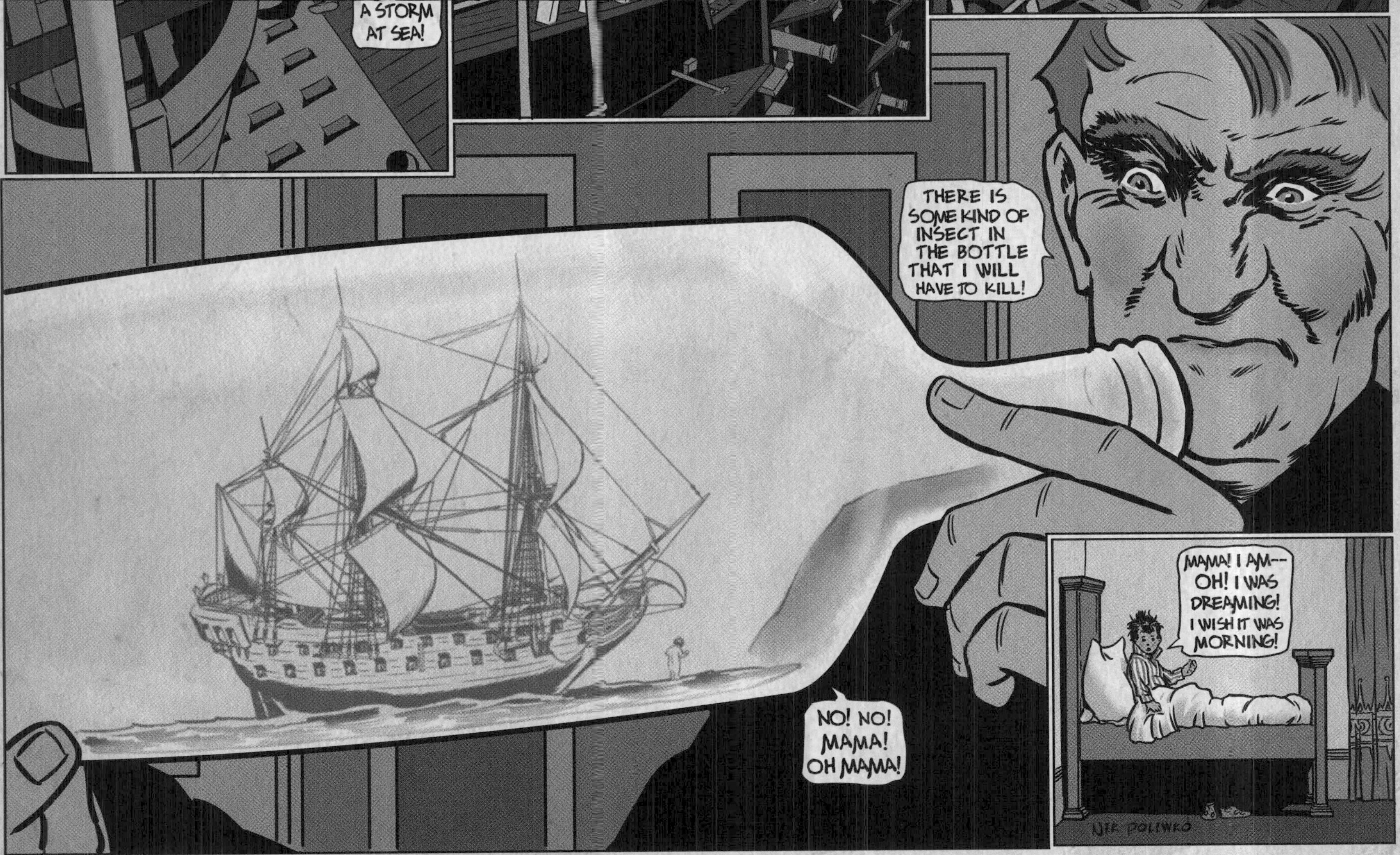
A STORM AT SEA!
THERE IS SOME KIND OF INSECT IN THE BOTTLE THAT I WILL HAVE TO KILL!
NO! NO! MAMA! OH MAMA!
MAMA! I AM-- OH! I WAS DREAMING! I WISH IT WAS MORNING!
NIK POLIWKO

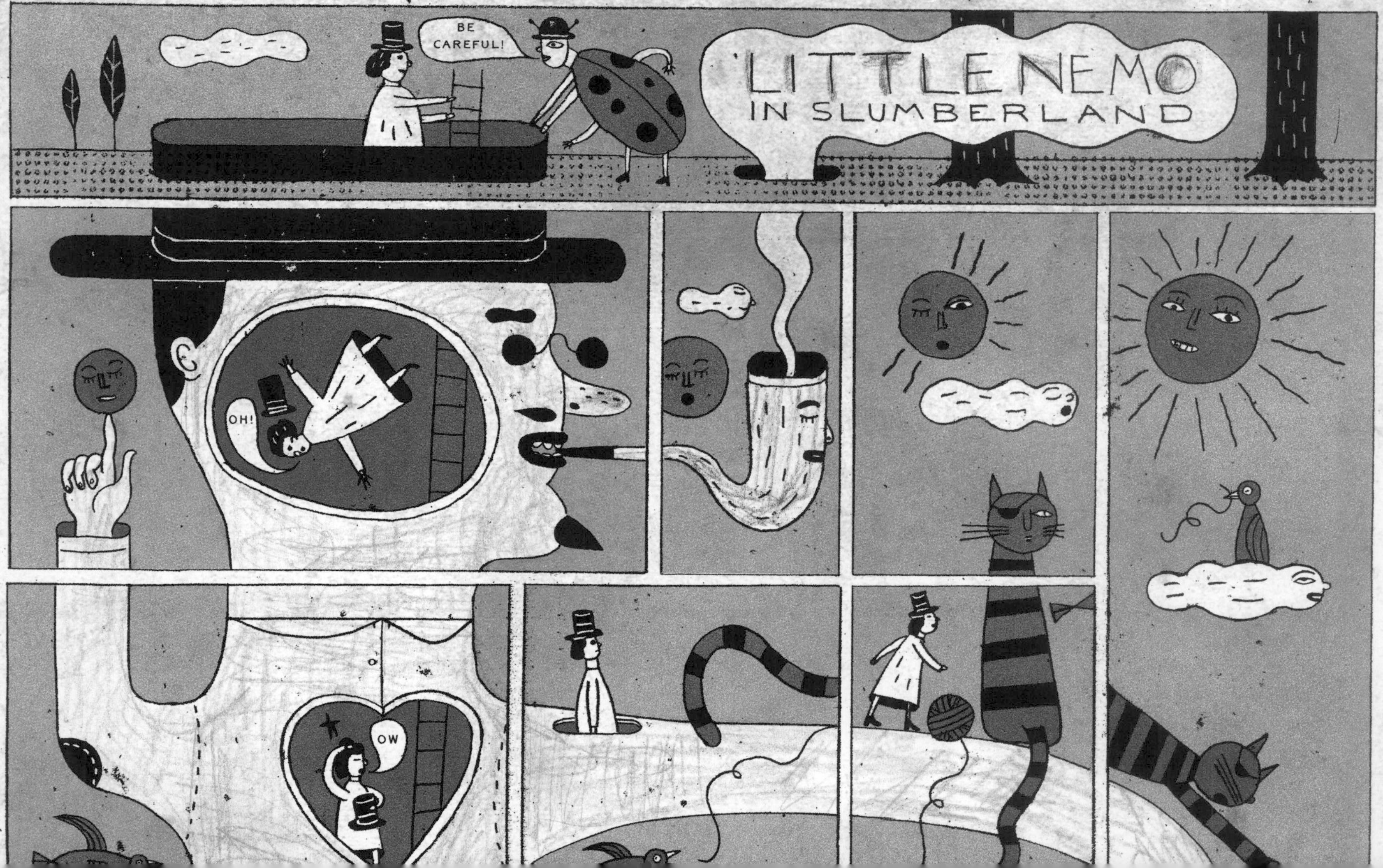
LITTLE NEMO
IN SLUMBERLAND
BE CAREFUL!
OH!
OW

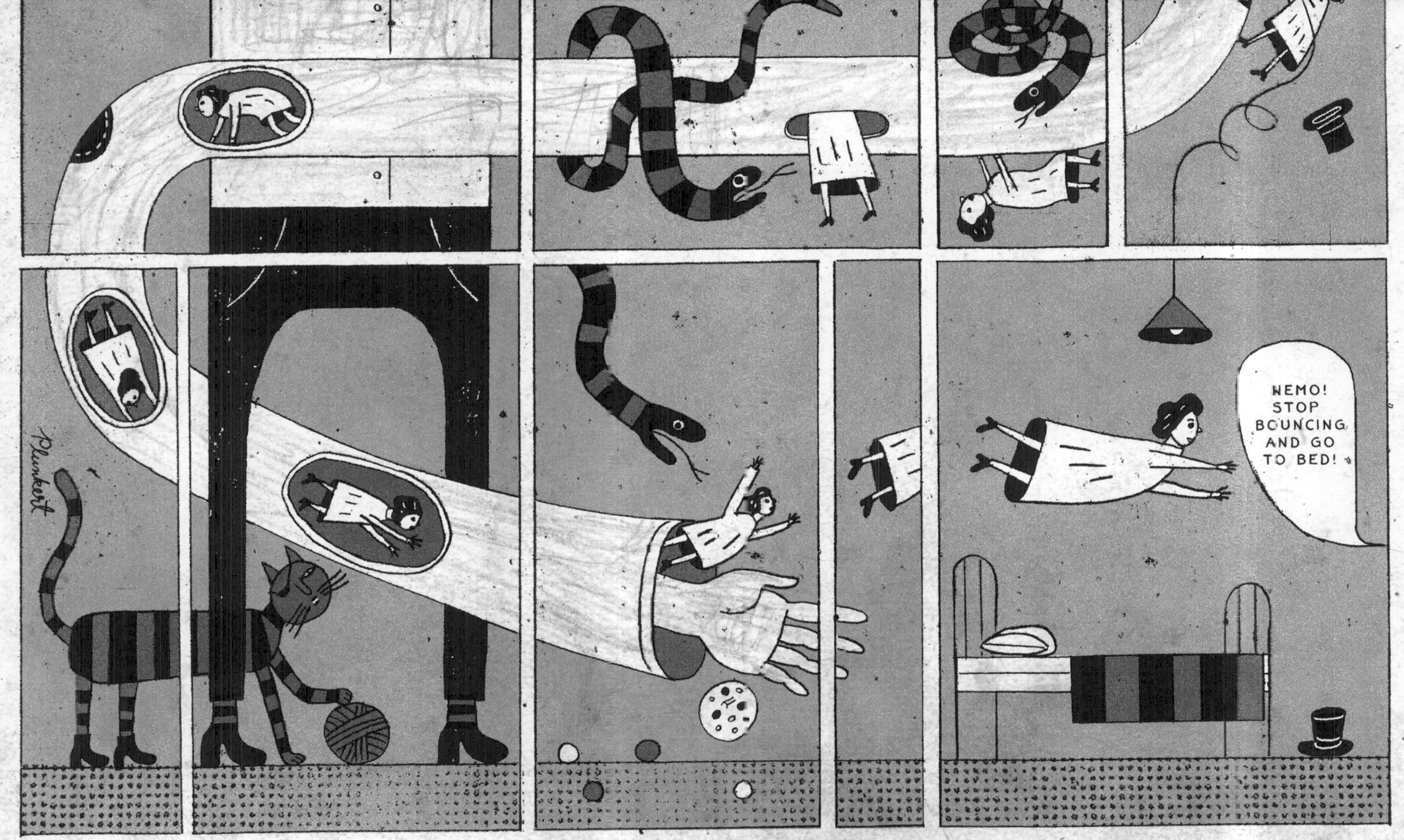
NEMO! STOP BOUNCING AND GO TO BED!
Plunkert

David Plunkert

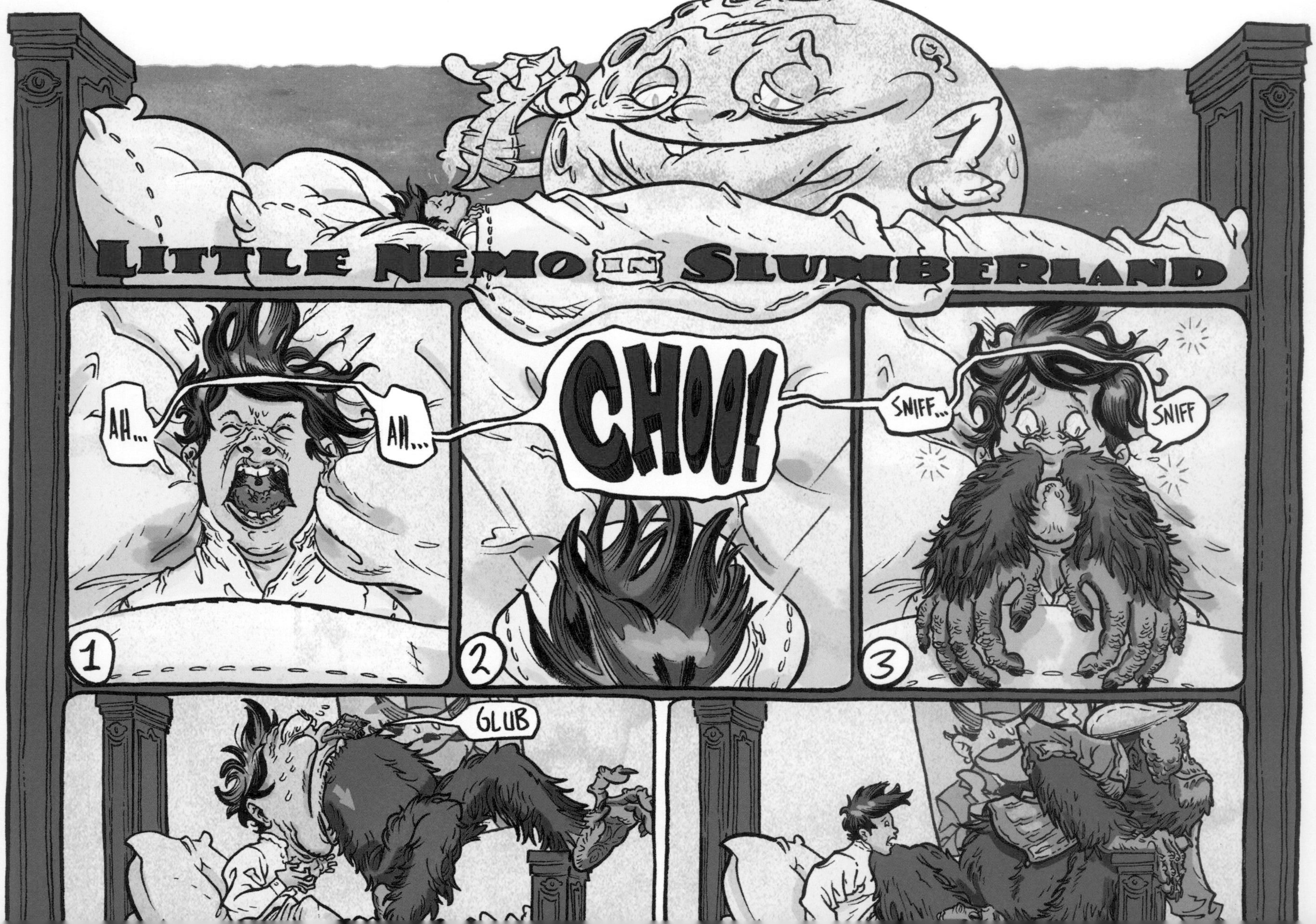
LITTLE NEMO IN SLUMBERLAND
1
AH...
AH...
2
CHOO!
3
SNIFF...
SNIFF
GLUB

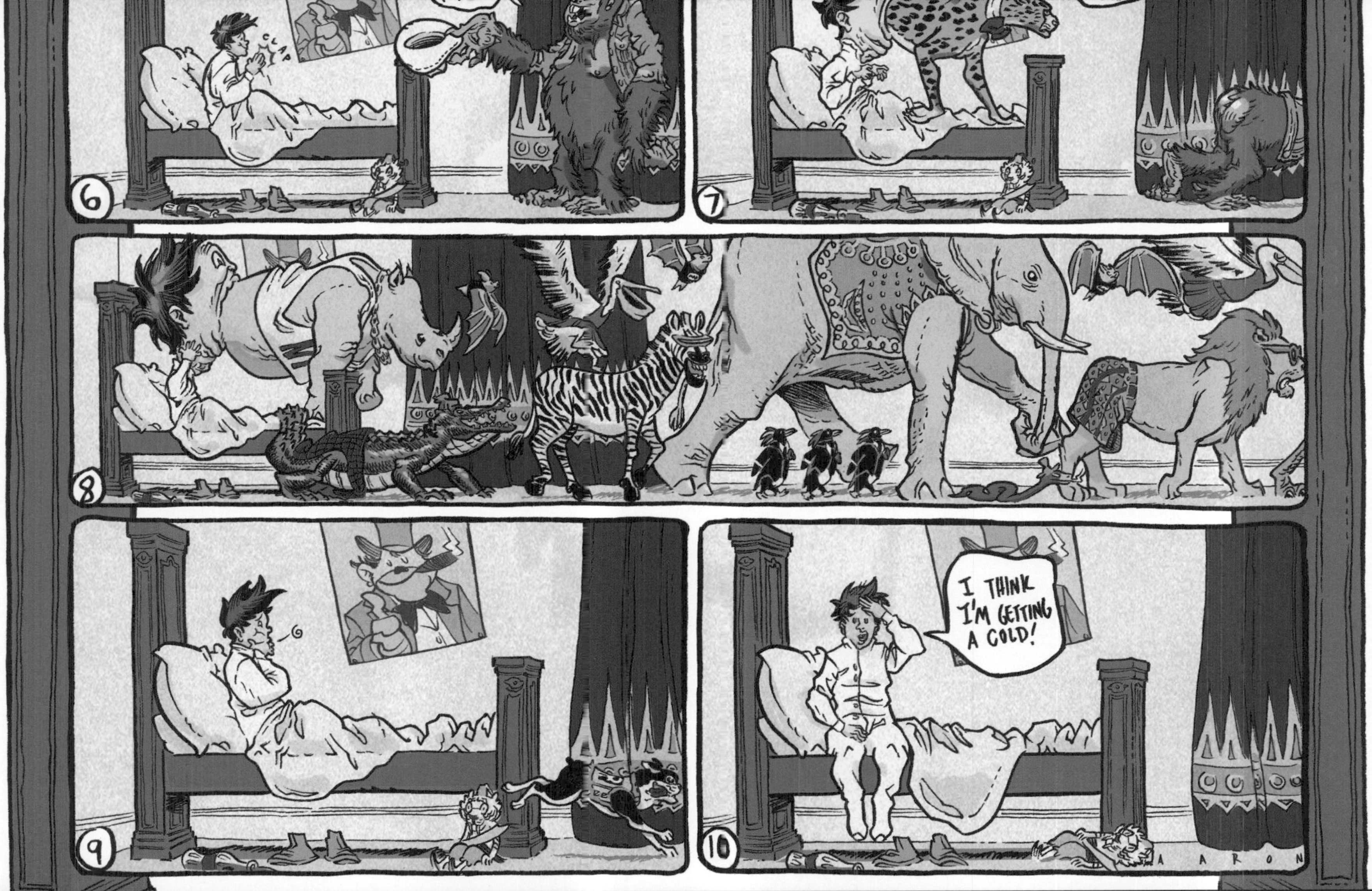
6
CLAP
7
8
9
10
I THINK I'M GETTING A COLD!
AARON

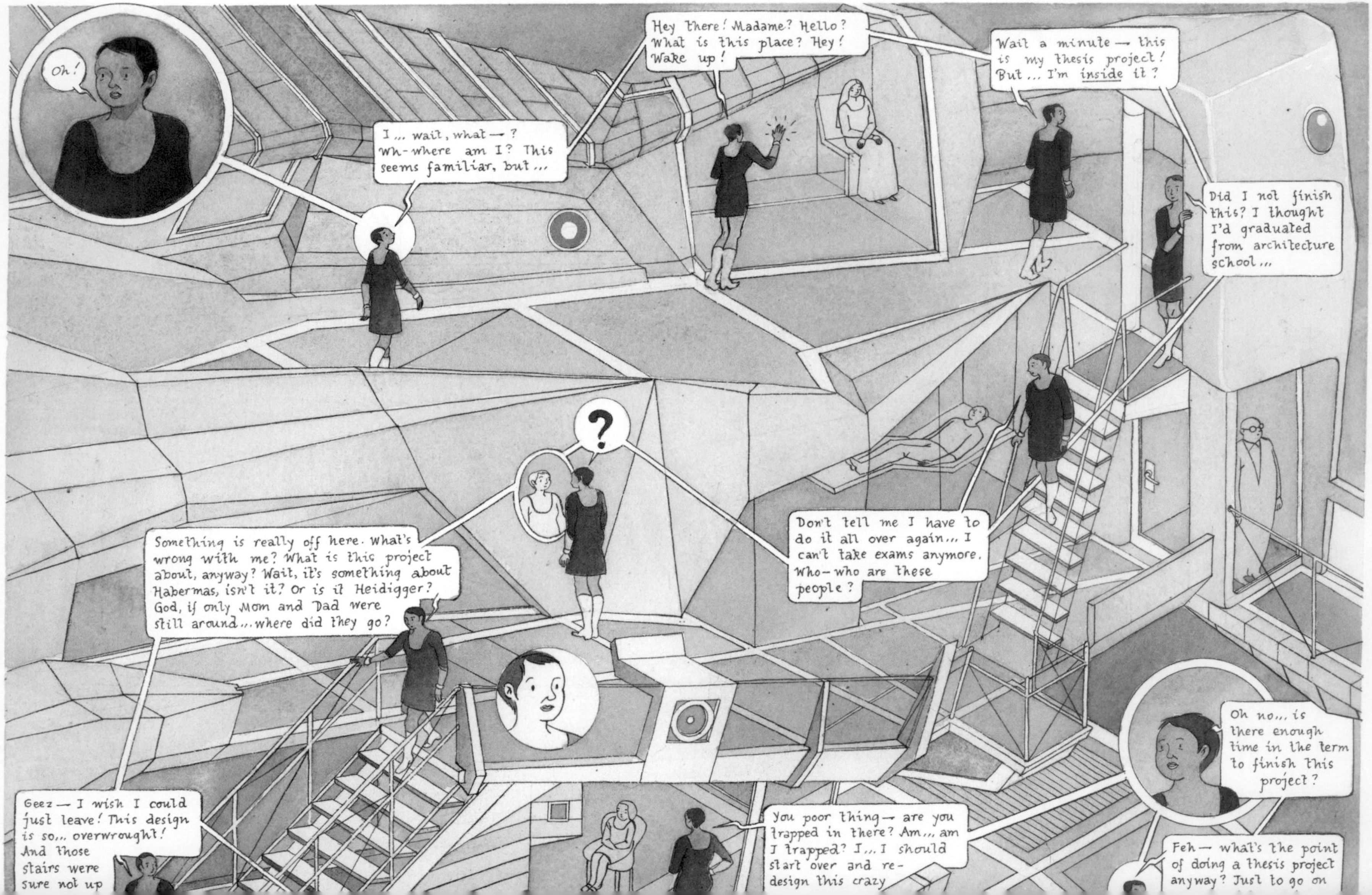
Oh!
I... wait, what—?
Wh-where am I? This seems familiar, but...
Hey there! Madame? Hello? What is this place? Hey! Wake up!
Wait a minute — this is my thesis project! But... I'm inside it?
Did I not finish this? I thought I'd graduated from architecture school...
?
Something is really off here. What's wrong with me? What is this project about, anyway? Wait, it's something about Habermas, isn't it? Or is it Heidigger? God, if only Mom and Dad were still around... where did they go?
Don't tell me I have to do it all over again... I can't take exams anymore. Who-who are these people?
Oh no... is there enough time in the term to finish this project?
Geez — I wish I could just leave! This design is so... overwrought! And those stairs were sure not up
You poor thing— are you trapped in there? Am... am I trapped? I... I should start over and re-design this crazy
Feh— what's the point of doing a thesis project anyway? Just to go on

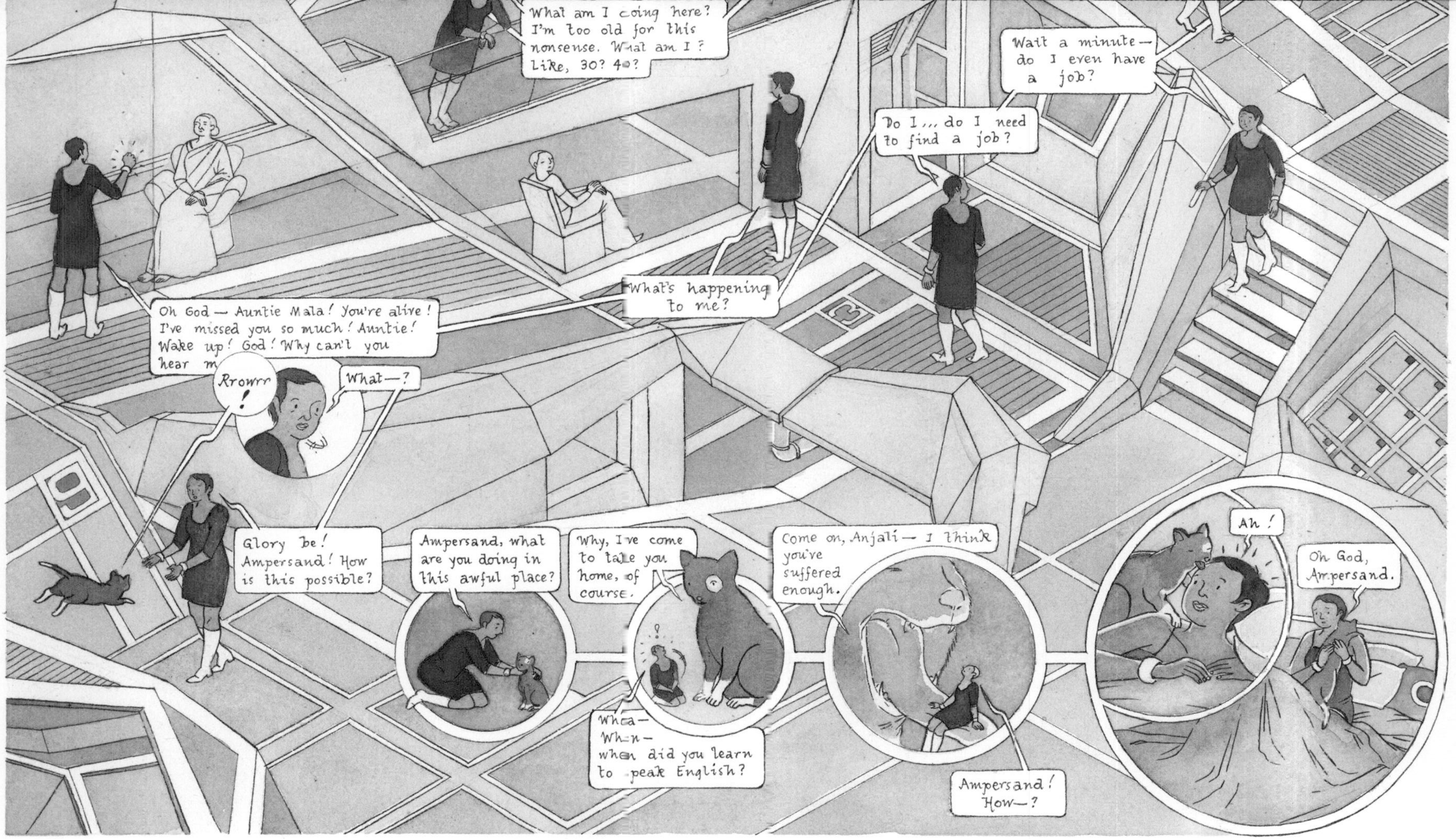
Oh God — Auntie Mala! You're alive! I've missed you so much! Auntie! Wake up! God! Why can't you hear m
What am I doing here? I'm too old for this nonsense. What am I? Like, 30? 40?
What's happening to me?
Do I... do I need to find a job?
Wait a minute — do I even have a job?
Rrowrr !
What—?
Glory be! Ampersand! How is this possible?
Ampersand, what are you doing in this awful place?
Why, I've come to take you home, of course.
Wha— Wh-n— when did you learn to speak English?
Come on, Anjali— I think you've suffered enough.
Ampersand! How—?
Ah!
Oh God, Ampersand.

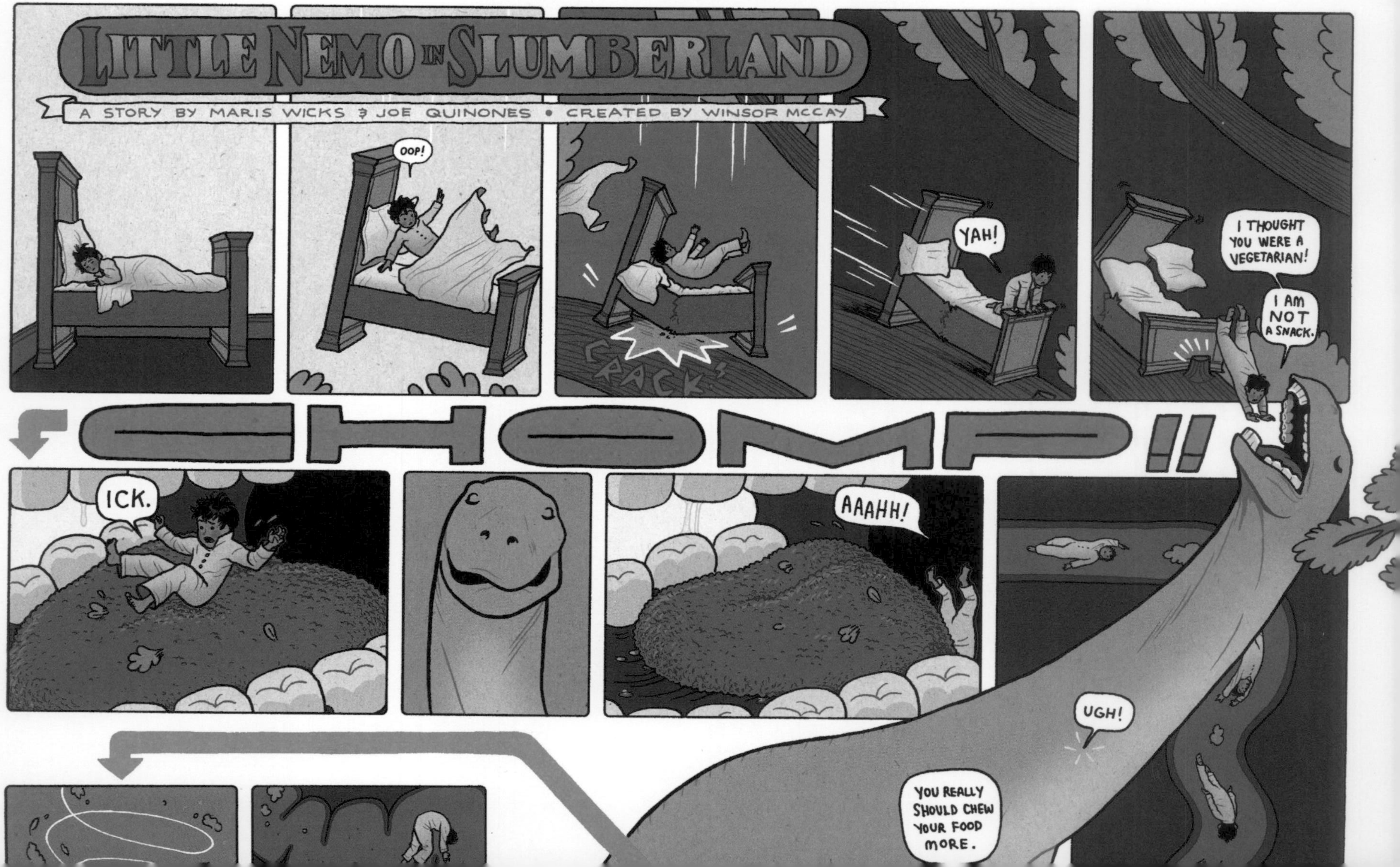
LITTLE NEMO IN SLUMBERLAND
A STORY BY MARIS WICKS & JOE QUINONES • CREATED BY WINSOR MCCAY
OOP!
CRACK!
YAH!
I THOUGHT YOU WERE A VEGETARIAN!
I AM NOT A SNACK.
CHOMP!!
ICK.
AAAHH!
UGH!
YOU REALLY SHOULD CHEW YOUR FOOD MORE.

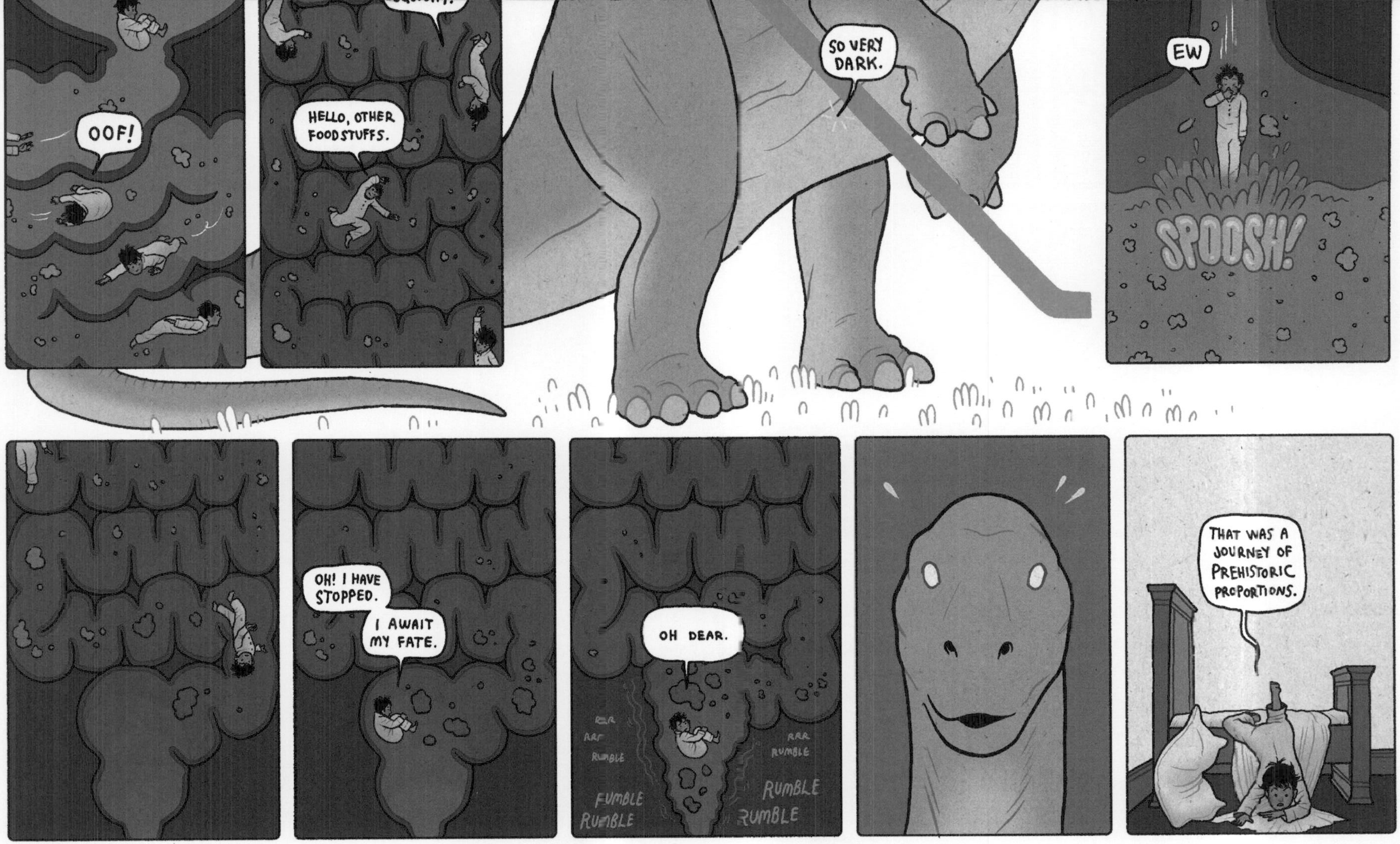
OOF!
HELLO, OTHER FOODSTUFFS.
SO VERY DARK.
EW
SPOOSH!
OH! I HAVE STOPPED.
I AWAIT MY FATE.
OH DEAR.
RRR
RRR
RUMBLE
FUMBLE
RUMBLE
RRR
RUMBLE
RUMBLE
RUMBLE
THAT WAS A JOURNEY OF PREHISTORIC PROPORTIONS.

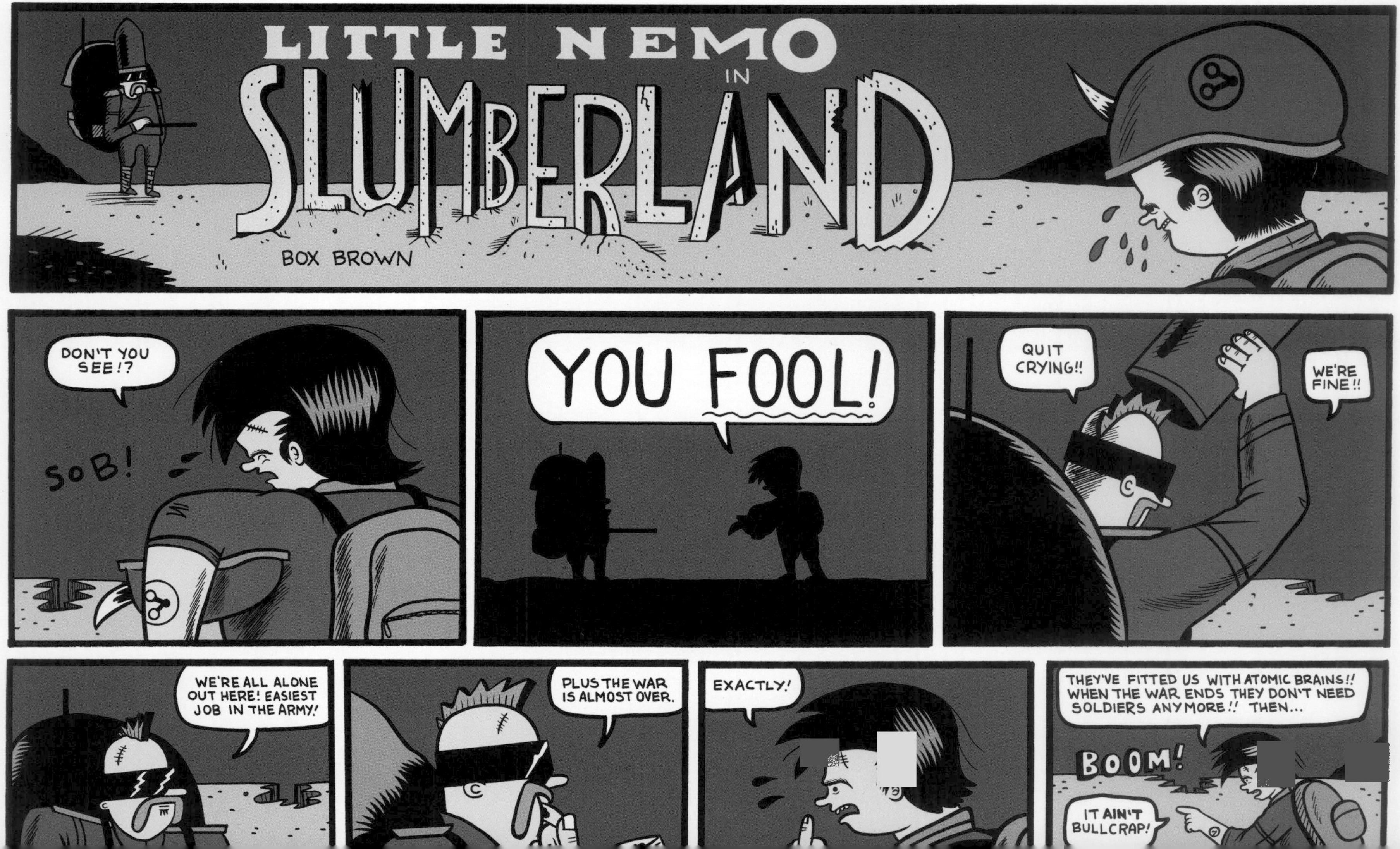
LITTLE NEMO IN SLUMBERLAND
BOX BROWN
DON'T YOU SEE!?
SOB!
YOU FOOL!
QUIT CRYING!!
WE'RE FINE!!
WE'RE ALL ALONE OUT HERE! EASIEST JOB IN THE ARMY!
PLUS THE WAR IS ALMOST OVER.
EXACTLY!
THEY'VE FITTED US WITH ATOMIC BRAINS!! WHEN THE WAR ENDS THEY DON'T NEED SOLDIERS ANYMORE!! THEN...
BOOM!
IT AIN'T BULLCRAP!

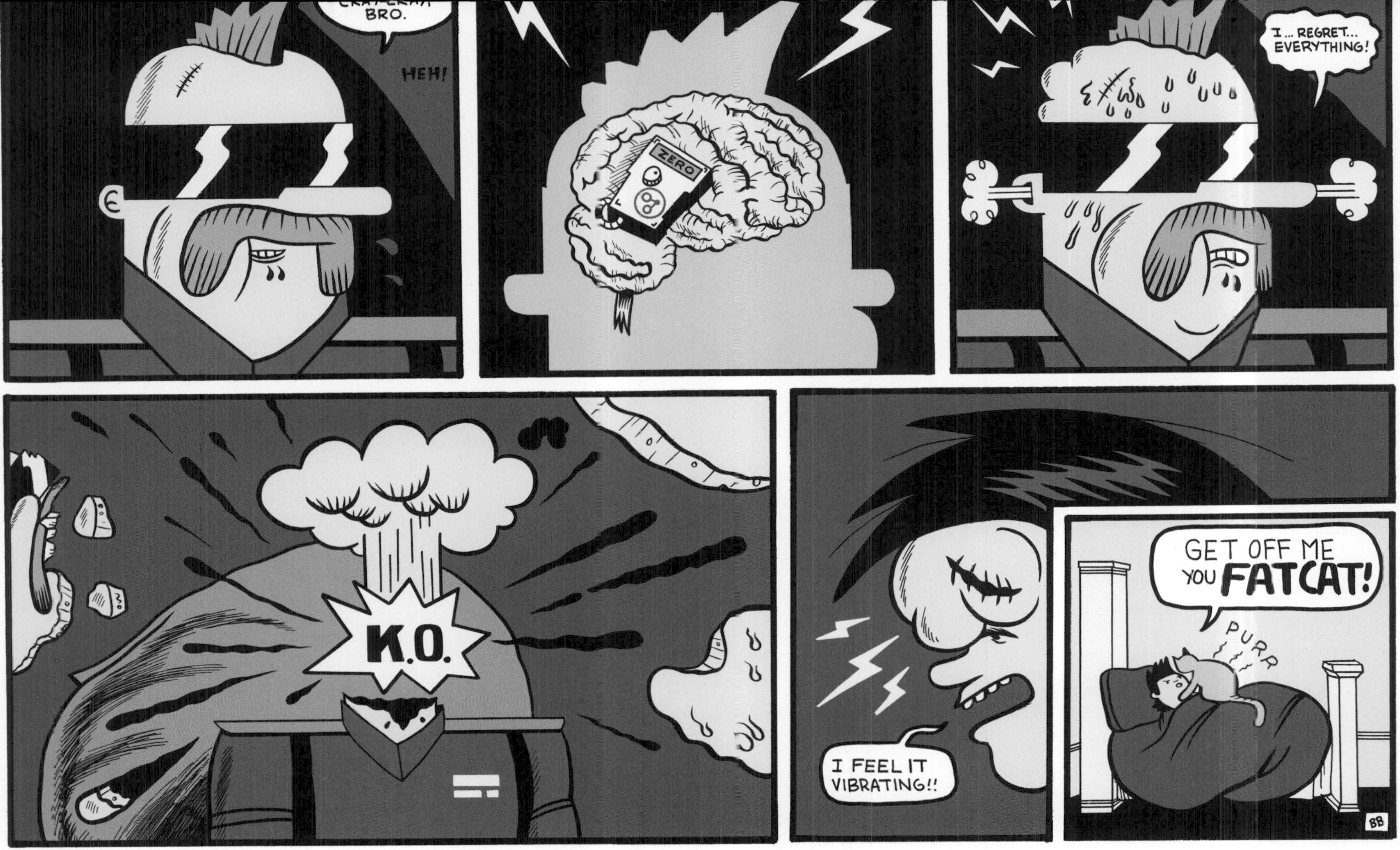
BRO.
HEH!
ZERO
I... REGRET... EVERYTHING!
K.O.
I FEEL IT VIBRATING!!
GET OFF ME YOU FATCAT!
PURR
BB

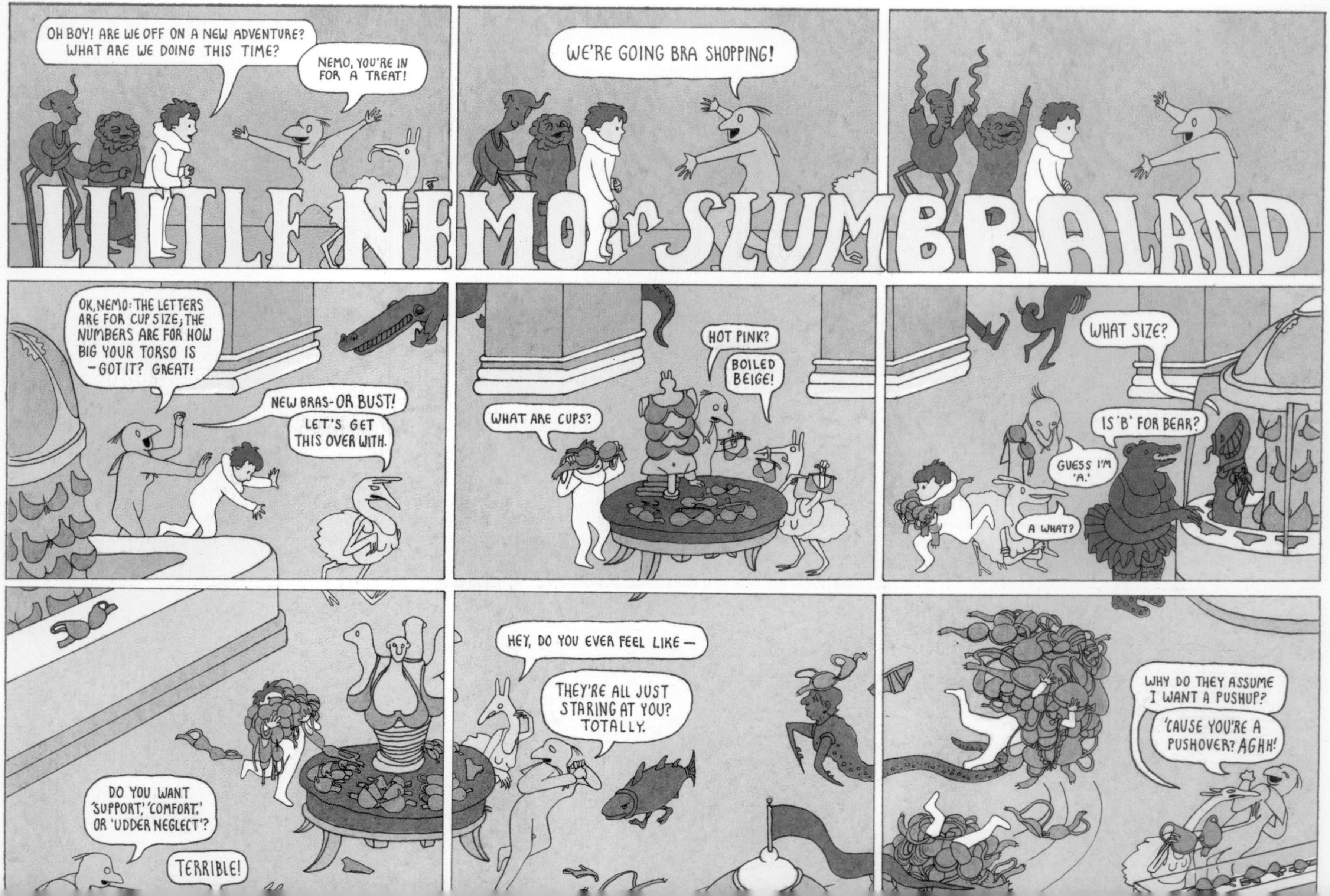
LITTLE NEMO in SLUMBRALAND
OH BOY! ARE WE OFF ON A NEW ADVENTURE? WHAT ARE WE DOING THIS TIME?
NEMO, YOU'RE IN FOR A TREAT!
WE'RE GOING BRA SHOPPING!
OK, NEMO: THE LETTERS ARE FOR CUP SIZE; THE NUMBERS ARE FOR HOW BIG YOUR TORSO IS – GOT IT? GREAT!
NEW BRAS-OR BUST!
LET'S GET THIS OVER WITH.
WHAT ARE CUPS?
HOT PINK?
BOILED BEIGE!
WHAT SIZE?
IS 'B' FOR BEAR?
GUESS I'M 'A.'
A WHAT?
DO YOU WANT 'SUPPORT,' 'COMFORT,' OR 'UDDER NEGLECT'?
TERRIBLE!
HEY, DO YOU EVER FEEL LIKE —
THEY'RE ALL JUST STARING AT YOU? TOTALLY.
WHY DO THEY ASSUME I WANT A PUSHUP?
'CAUSE YOU'RE A PUSHOVER? AGHH!

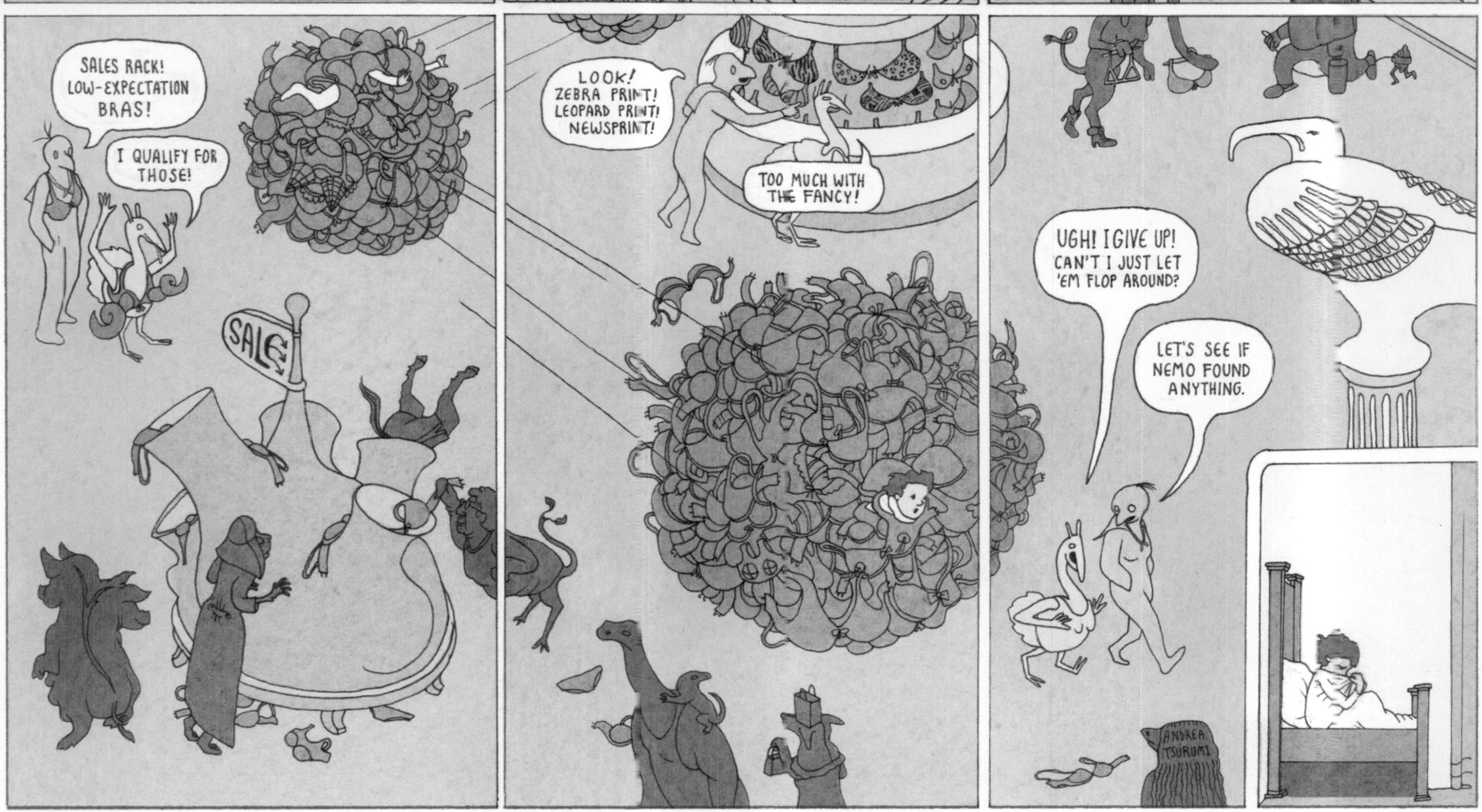
SALES RACK! LOW-EXPECTATION BRAS!
I QUALIFY FOR THOSE!
SALE
LOOK! ZEBRA PRINT! LEOPARD PRINT! NEWSPRINT!
TOO MUCH WITH THE FANCY!
UGH! I GIVE UP! CAN'T I JUST LET 'EM FLOP AROUND?
LET'S SEE IF NEMO FOUND ANYTHING.
ANDREA TSURUMI

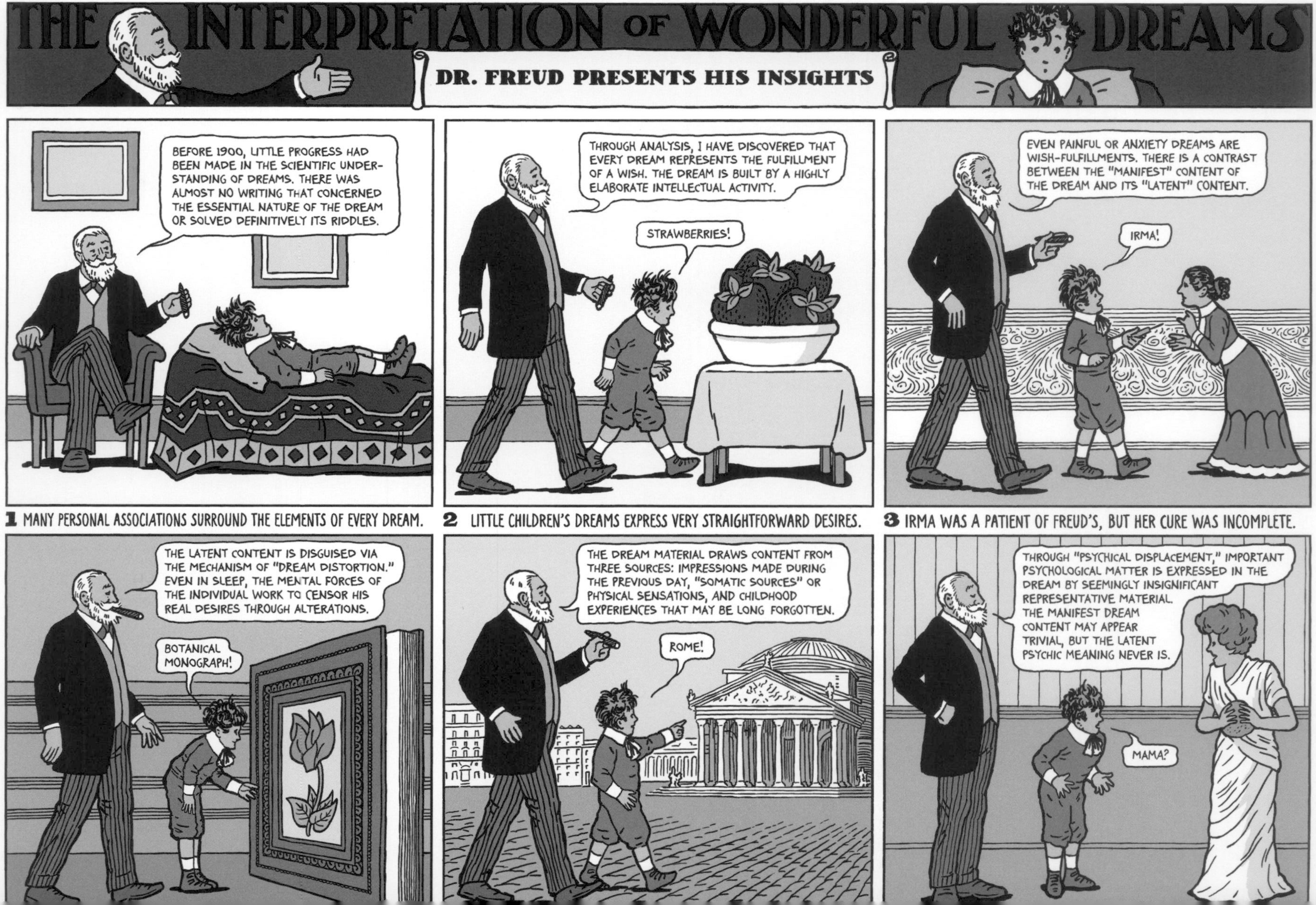
THE INTERPRETATION OF WONDERFUL DREAMS
DR. FREUD PRESENTS HIS INSIGHTS
BEFORE 1900, LITTLE PROGRESS HAD BEEN MADE IN THE SCIENTIFIC UNDERSTANDING OF DREAMS. THERE WAS ALMOST NO WRITING THAT CONCERNED THE ESSENTIAL NATURE OF THE DREAM OR SOLVED DEFINITIVELY ITS RIDDLES.
1 MANY PERSONAL ASSOCIATIONS SURROUND THE ELEMENTS OF EVERY DREAM.
THROUGH ANALYSIS, I HAVE DISCOVERED THAT EVERY DREAM REPRESENTS THE FULFILLMENT OF A WISH. THE DREAM IS BUILT BY A HIGHLY ELABORATE INTELLECTUAL ACTIVITY.
STRAWBERRIES!
2 LITTLE CHILDREN'S DREAMS EXPRESS VERY STRAIGHTFORWARD DESIRES.
EVEN PAINFUL OR ANXIETY DREAMS ARE WISH-FULFILLMENTS. THERE IS A CONTRAST BETWEEN THE "MANIFEST" CONTENT OF THE DREAM AND ITS "LATENT" CONTENT.
IRMA!
3 IRMA WAS A PATIENT OF FREUD'S, BUT HER CURE WAS INCOMPLETE.
THE LATENT CONTENT IS DISGUISED VIA THE MECHANISM OF "DREAM DISTORTION." EVEN IN SLEEP, THE MENTAL FORCES OF THE INDIVIDUAL WORK TO CENSOR HIS REAL DESIRES THROUGH ALTERATIONS.
BOTANICAL MONOGRAPH!
THE DREAM MATERIAL DRAWS CONTENT FROM THREE SOURCES: IMPRESSIONS MADE DURING THE PREVIOUS DAY, "SOMATIC SOURCES" OR PHYSICAL SENSATIONS, AND CHILDHOOD EXPERIENCES THAT MAY BE LONG FORGOTTEN.
ROME!
THROUGH "PSYCHICAL DISPLACEMENT," IMPORTANT PSYCHOLOGICAL MATTER IS EXPRESSED IN THE DREAM BY SEEMINGLY INSIGNIFICANT REPRESENTATIVE MATERIAL. THE MANIFEST DREAM CONTENT MAY APPEAR TRIVIAL, BUT THE LATENT PSYCHIC MEANING NEVER IS.
MAMA?

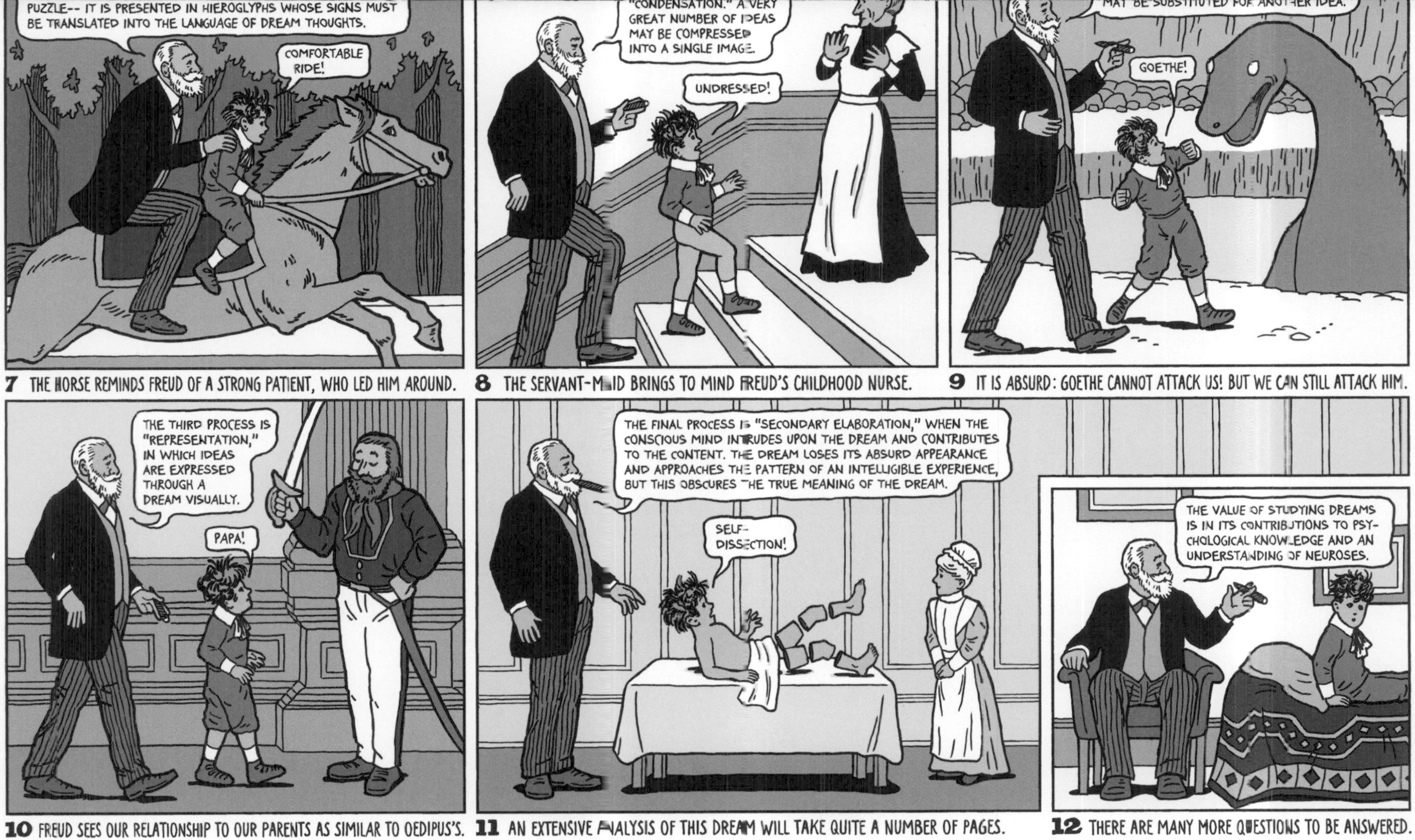
PUZZLE-- IT IS PRESENTED IN HIEROGLYPHS WHOSE SIGNS MUST BE TRANSLATED INTO THE LANGUAGE OF DREAM THOUGHTS.
COMFORTABLE RIDE!
7 THE HORSE REMINDS FREUD OF A STRONG PATIENT, WHO LED HIM AROUND.
"CONDENSATION." A VERY GREAT NUMBER OF IDEAS MAY BE COMPRESSED INTO A SINGLE IMAGE.
UNDRESSED!
8 THE SERVANT-MAID BRINGS TO MIND FREUD'S CHILDHOOD NURSE.
GOETHE!
9 IT IS ABSURD: GOETHE CANNOT ATTACK US! BUT WE CAN STILL ATTACK HIM.
THE THIRD PROCESS IS "REPRESENTATION," IN WHICH IDEAS ARE EXPRESSED THROUGH A DREAM VISUALLY.
PAPA!
10 FREUD SEES OUR RELATIONSHIP TO OUR PARENTS AS SIMILAR TO OEDIPUS'S.
THE FINAL PROCESS IS "SECONDARY ELABORATION," WHEN THE CONSCIOUS MIND INTRUDES UPON THE DREAM AND CONTRIBUTES TO THE CONTENT. THE DREAM LOSES ITS ABSURD APPEARANCE AND APPROACHES THE PATTERN OF AN INTELLIGIBLE EXPERIENCE, BUT THIS OBSCURES THE TRUE MEANING OF THE DREAM.
SELF-DISSECTION!
11 AN EXTENSIVE ANALYSIS OF THIS DREAM WILL TAKE QUITE A NUMBER OF PAGES.
THE VALUE OF STUDYING DREAMS IS IN ITS CONTRIBUTIONS TO PSYCHOLOGICAL KNOWLEDGE AND AN UNDERSTANDING OF NEUROSES.
12 THERE ARE MANY MORE QUESTIONS TO BE ANSWERED.

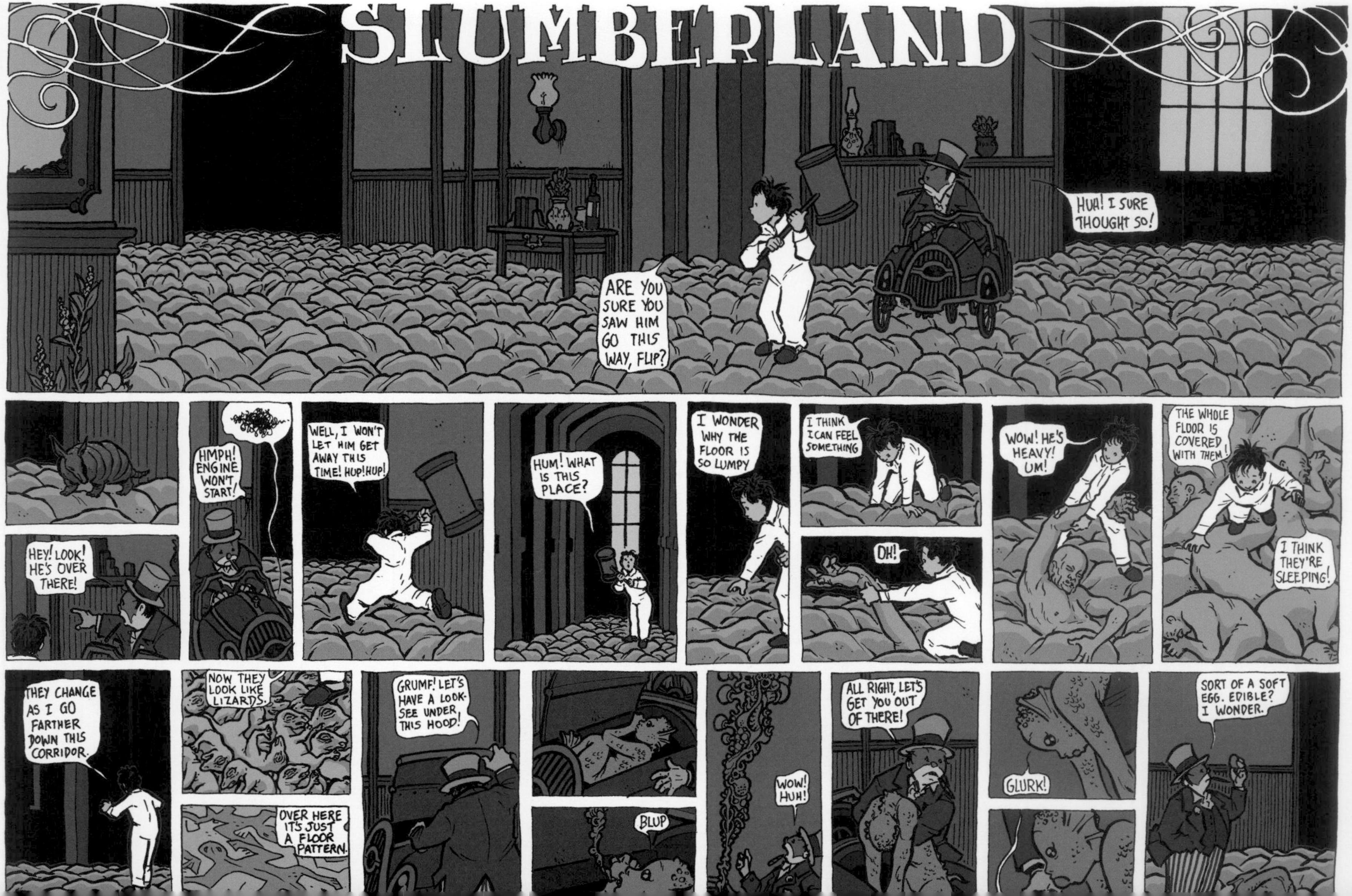
SLUMBERLAND
ARE YOU SURE YOU SAW HIM GO THIS WAY, FLIP?
HUH! I SURE THOUGHT SO!
HEY! LOOK! HE'S OVER THERE!
HMPH! ENGINE WON'T START!
WELL, I WON'T LET HIM GET AWAY THIS TIME! HUP! HUP!
HUM! WHAT IS THIS PLACE?
I WONDER WHY THE FLOOR IS SO LUMPY
I THINK I CAN FEEL SOMETHING
OH!
WOW! HE'S HEAVY! UM!
THE WHOLE FLOOR IS COVERED WITH THEM!
I THINK THEY'RE SLEEPING!
THEY CHANGE AS I GO FARTHER DOWN THIS CORRIDOR.
NOW THEY LOOK LIKE LIZARDS.
OVER HERE IT'S JUST A FLOOR PATTERN.
GRUMF! LET'S HAVE A LOOK-SEE UNDER THIS HOOD!
BLUP
WOW! HUH!
ALL RIGHT, LET'S GET YOU OUT OF THERE!
GLURK!
SORT OF A SOFT EGG. EDIBLE? I WONDER.

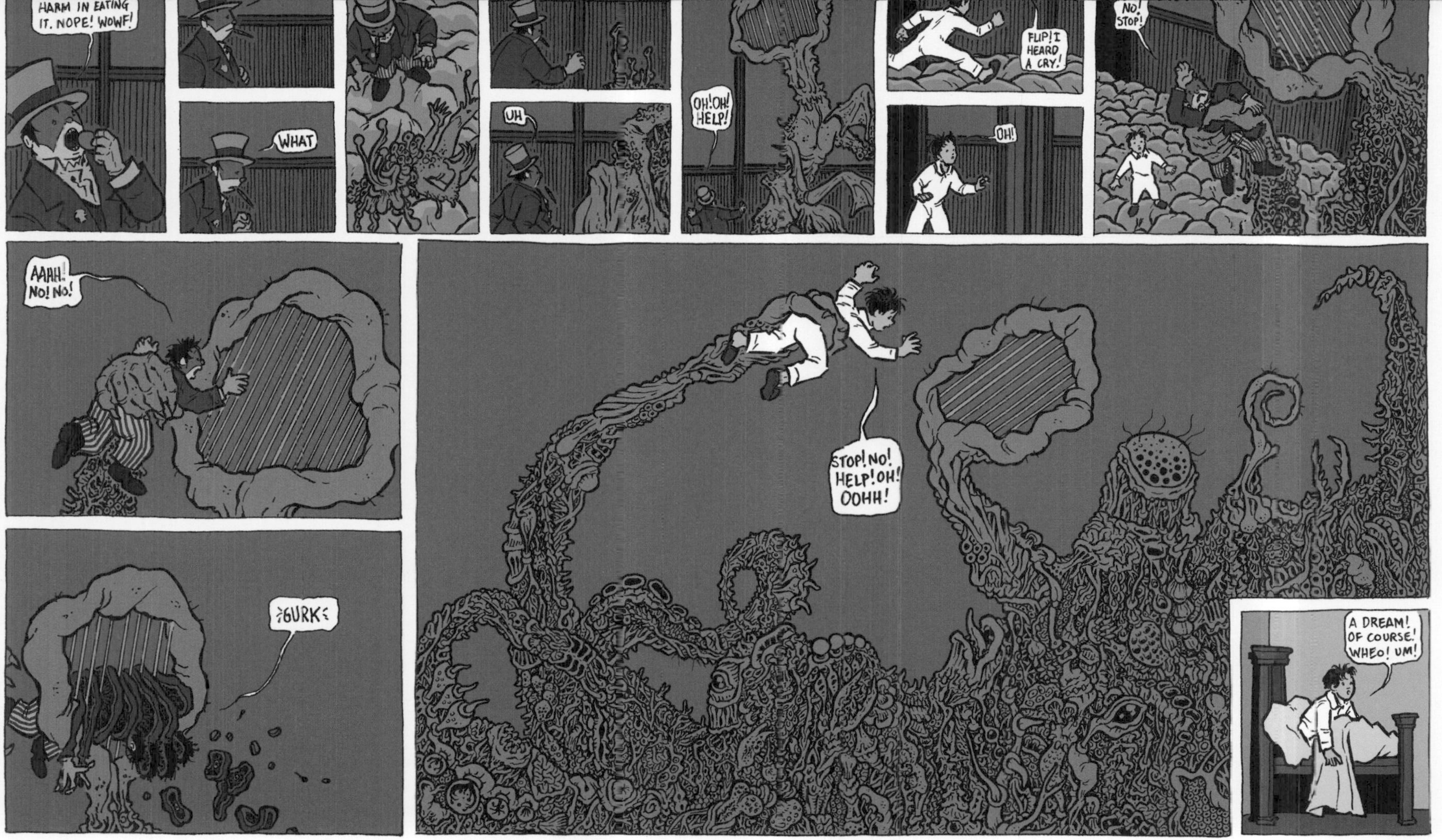
HARM IN EATING IT. NOPE! WOWF!
WHAT
UH
OH! OH! HELP!
FLIP! I HEARD A CRY!
OH!
NO! STOP!
AAHH! NO! NO!
GURK
STOP! NO! HELP! OH! OOHH!
A DREAM! OF COURSE! WHEO! UM!

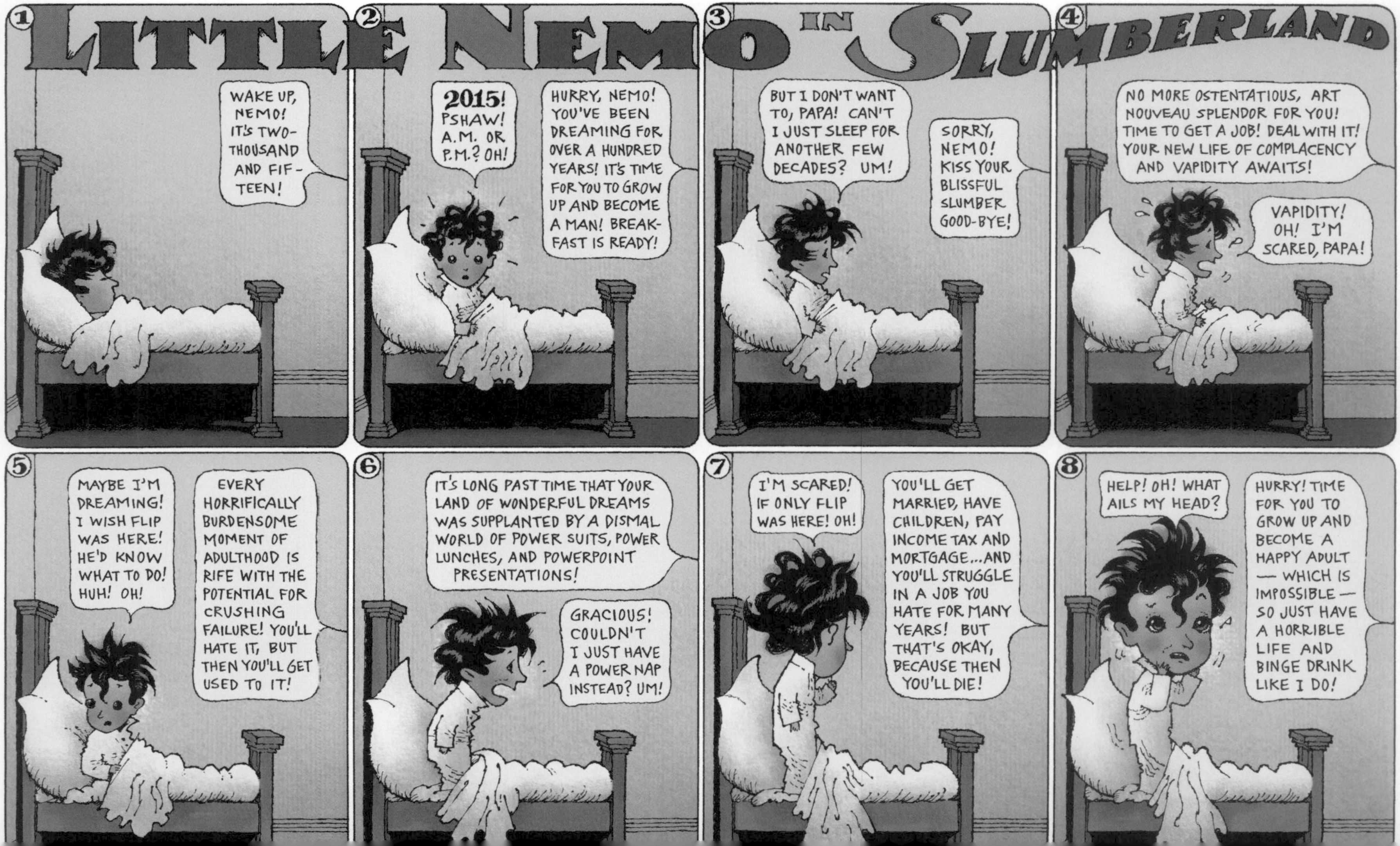
LITTLE NEMO IN SLUMBERLAND
1
WAKE UP, NEMO! IT'S TWO-THOUSAND AND FIF-TEEN!
2
2015! PSHAW! A.M. OR P.M.? OH!
HURRY, NEMO! YOU'VE BEEN DREAMING FOR OVER A HUNDRED YEARS! IT'S TIME FOR YOU TO GROW UP AND BECOME A MAN! BREAK-FAST IS READY!
3
BUT I DON'T WANT TO, PAPA! CAN'T I JUST SLEEP FOR ANOTHER FEW DECADES? UM!
SORRY, NEMO! KISS YOUR BLISSFUL SLUMBER GOOD-BYE!
4
NO MORE OSTENTATIOUS, ART NOUVEAU SPLENDOR FOR YOU! TIME TO GET A JOB! DEAL WITH IT! YOUR NEW LIFE OF COMPLACENCY AND VAPIDITY AWAITS!
VAPIDITY! OH! I'M SCARED, PAPA!
5
MAYBE I'M DREAMING! I WISH FLIP WAS HERE! HE'D KNOW WHAT TO DO! HUH! OH!
EVERY HORRIFICALLY BURDENSOME MOMENT OF ADULTHOOD IS RIFE WITH THE POTENTIAL FOR CRUSHING FAILURE! YOU'LL HATE IT, BUT THEN YOU'LL GET USED TO IT!
6
IT'S LONG PAST TIME THAT YOUR LAND OF WONDERFUL DREAMS WAS SUPPLANTED BY A DISMAL WORLD OF POWER SUITS, POWER LUNCHES, AND POWERPOINT PRESENTATIONS!
GRACIOUS! COULDN'T I JUST HAVE A POWER NAP INSTEAD? UM!
7
I'M SCARED! IF ONLY FLIP WAS HERE! OH!
YOU'LL GET MARRIED, HAVE CHILDREN, PAY INCOME TAX AND MORTGAGE...AND YOU'LL STRUGGLE IN A JOB YOU HATE FOR MANY YEARS! BUT THAT'S OKAY, BECAUSE THEN YOU'LL DIE!
8
HELP! OH! WHAT AILS MY HEAD?
HURRY! TIME FOR YOU TO GROW UP AND BECOME A HAPPY ADULT — WHICH IS IMPOSSIBLE — SO JUST HAVE A HORRIBLE LIFE AND BINGE DRINK LIKE I DO!

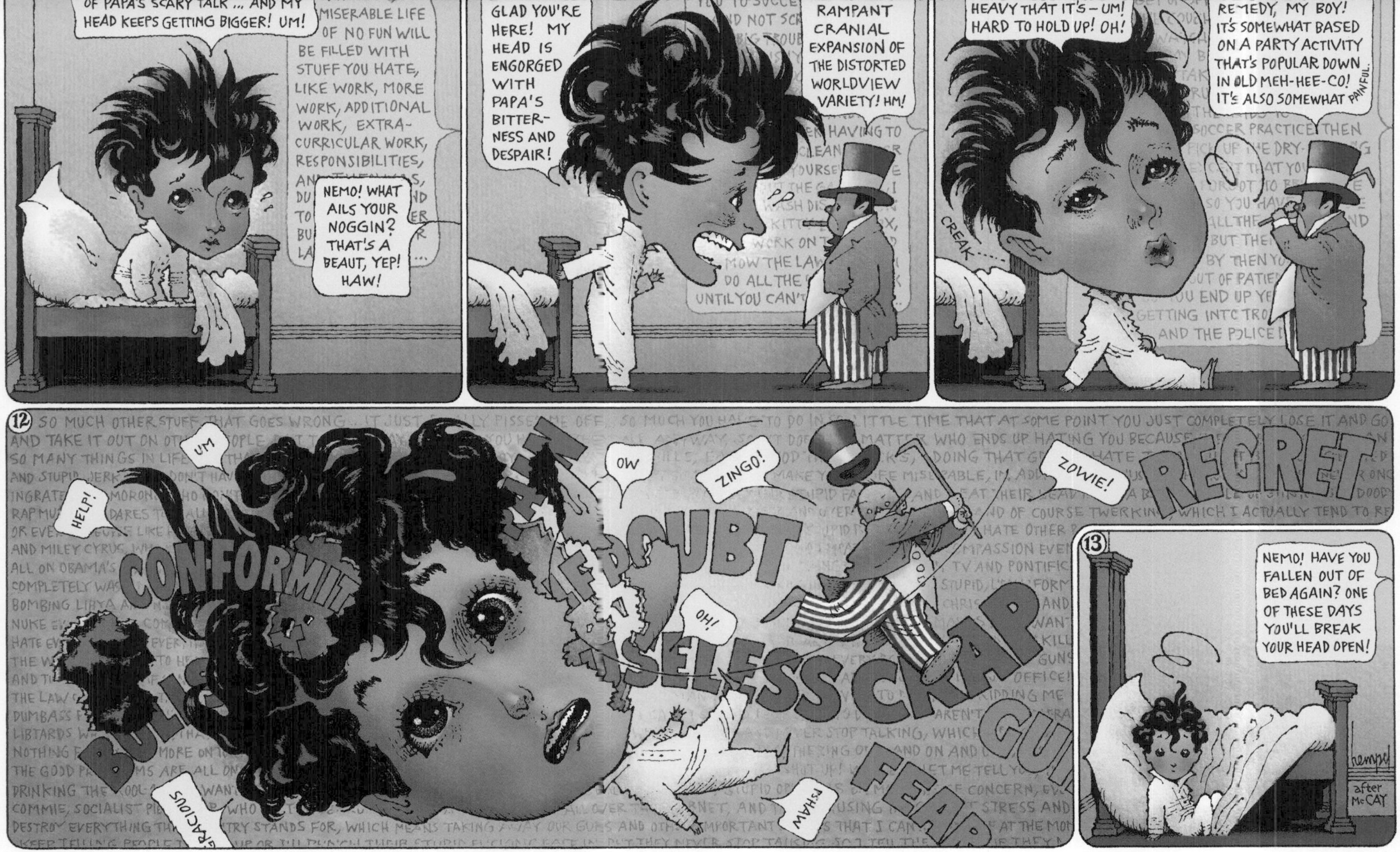

OF PAPA'S SCARY TALK ... AND MY HEAD KEEPS GETTING BIGGER! UM!
MISERABLE LIFE OF NO FUN WILL BE FILLED WITH STUFF YOU HATE, LIKE WORK, MORE WORK, ADDITIONAL WORK, EXTRA-CURRICULAR WORK, RESPONSIBILITIES,
NEMO! WHAT AILS YOUR NOGGIN? THAT'S A BEAUT, YEP! HAW!
GLAD YOU'RE HERE! MY HEAD IS ENGORGED WITH PAPA'S BITTERNESS AND DESPAIR!
RAMPANT CRANIAL EXPANSION OF THE DISTORTED WORLDVIEW VARIETY! HM!
HEAVY THAT IT'S – UM! HARD TO HOLD UP! OH!
REMEDY, MY BOY! IT'S SOMEWHAT BASED ON A PARTY ACTIVITY THAT'S POPULAR DOWN IN OLD MEH-HEE-CO! IT'S ALSO SOMEWHAT PAINFUL.
CREAK
12
UM
HELP!
OW
ZINGO!
ZOWIE!
OH!
PSHAW
GRACIOUS
CONFORMIT
DOUBT
USELESS
CRAP
REGRET
FEAR
13
NEMO! HAVE YOU FALLEN OUT OF BED AGAIN? ONE OF THESE DAYS YOU'LL BREAK YOUR HEAD OPEN!
hempel after McCAY

Marc Hempel

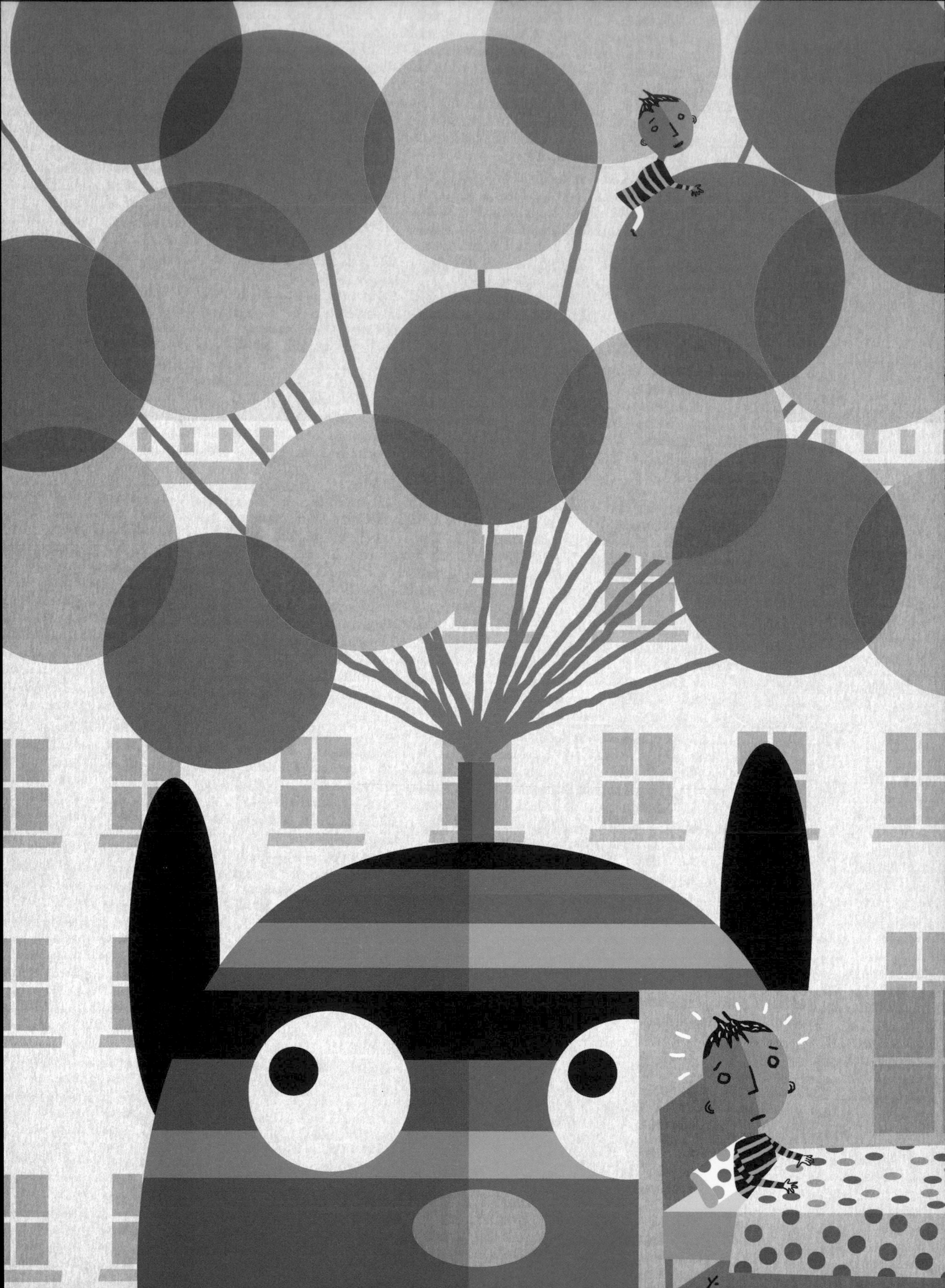

James Yang

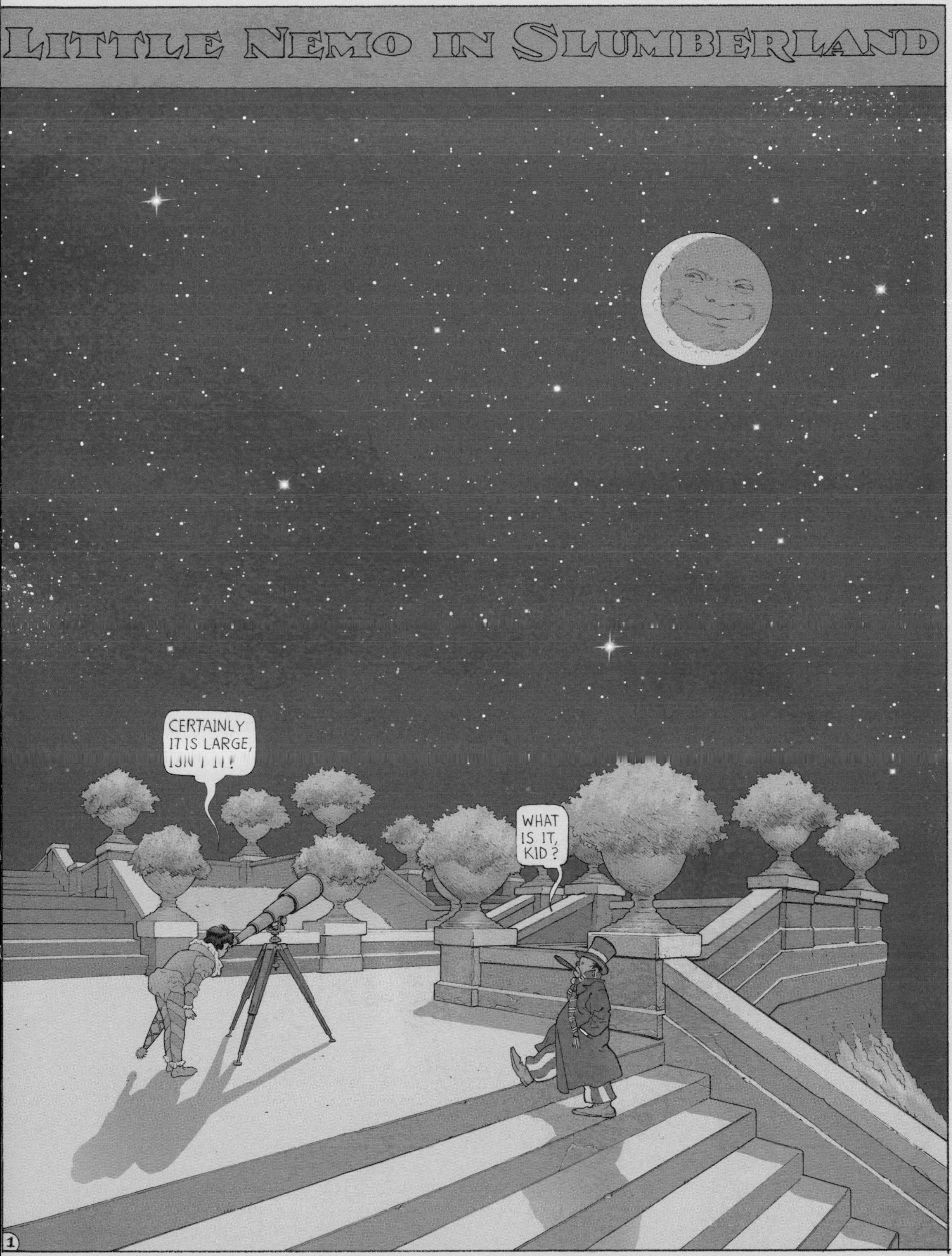
LITTLE NEMO IN SLUMBERLAND
CERTAINLY IT IS LARGE,
WHAT IS IT, KID?
1

J. G. Jones

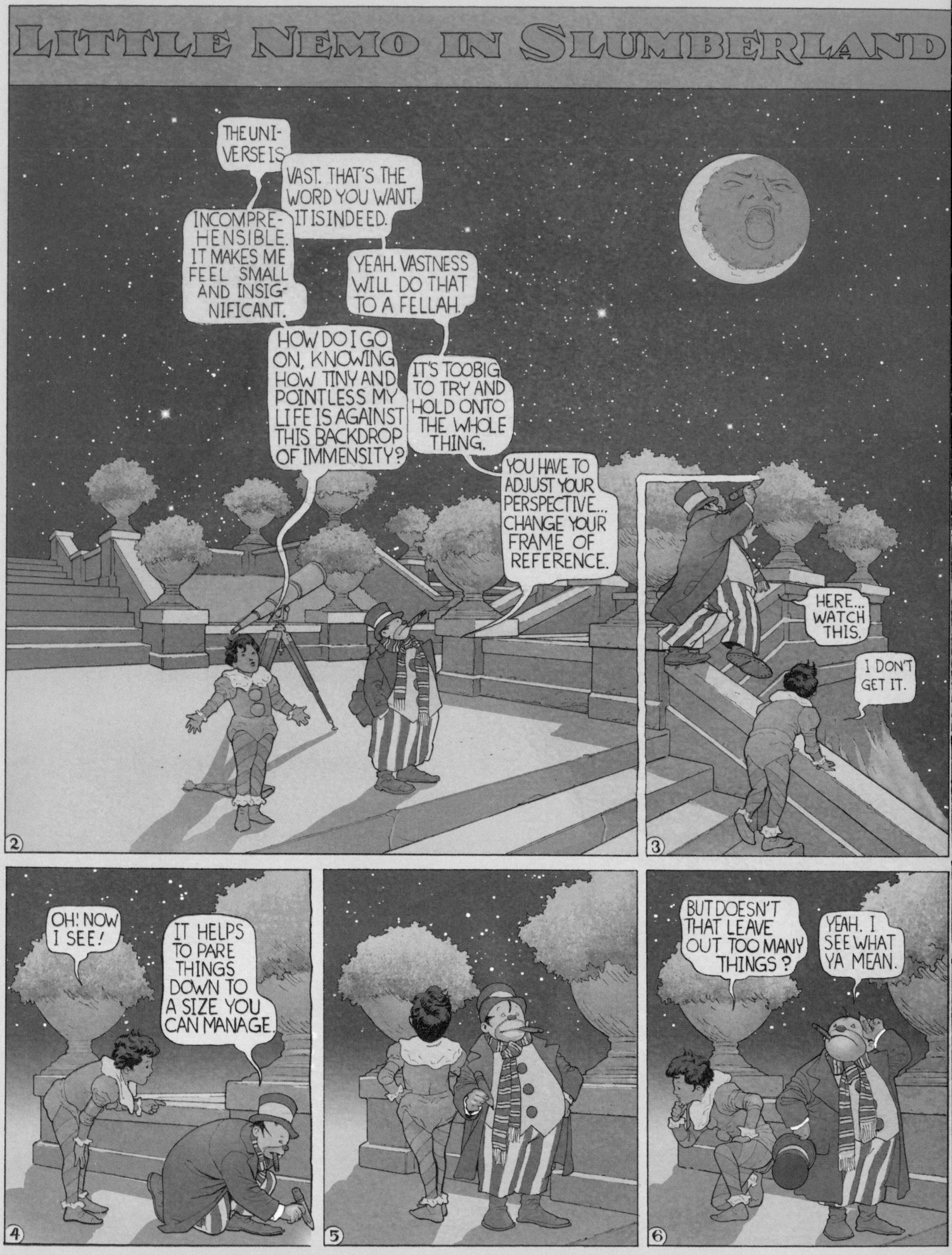
LITTLE NEMO IN SLUMBERLAND
THE UNI-VERSE IS
VAST. THAT'S THE WORD YOU WANT. IT IS INDEED.
INCOMPRE-HENSIBLE. IT MAKES ME FEEL SMALL AND INSIG-NIFICANT.
YEAH. VASTNESS WILL DO THAT TO A FELLAH.
HOW DO I GO ON, KNOWING HOW TINY AND POINTLESS MY LIFE IS AGAINST THIS BACKDROP OF IMMENSITY?
IT'S TOO BIG TO TRY AND HOLD ONTO THE WHOLE THING.
YOU HAVE TO ADJUST YOUR PERSPECTIVE... CHANGE YOUR FRAME OF REFERENCE.
2
HERE... WATCH THIS.
I DON'T GET IT.
3
OH! NOW I SEE!
IT HELPS TO PARE THINGS DOWN TO A SIZE YOU CAN MANAGE.
4
5
BUT DOESN'T THAT LEAVE OUT TOO MANY THINGS?
YEAH. I SEE WHAT YA MEAN.
6

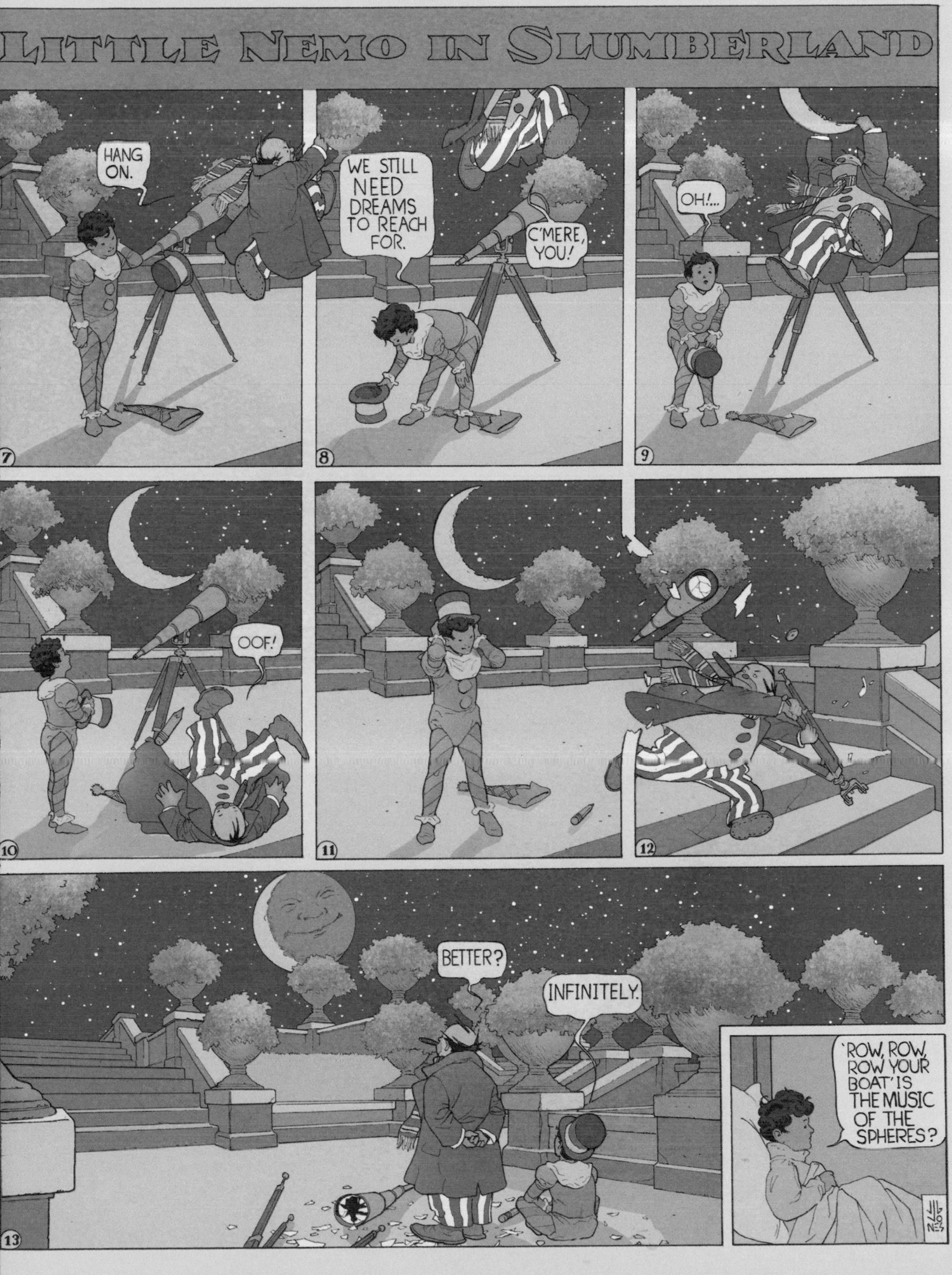
LITTLE NEMO IN SLUMBERLAND
HANG ON.
WE STILL NEED DREAMS TO REACH FOR.
C'MERE, YOU!
OH!...
OOF!
BETTER?
INFINITELY.
'ROW, ROW, ROW YOUR BOAT' IS THE MUSIC OF THE SPHERES?

AAAIII-IIEEE!
12
Jim Rugg

AAA-AIIII-IEEE-EEE!!!

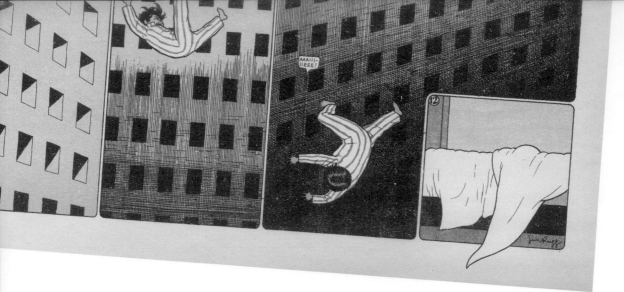

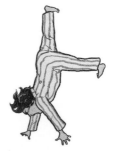

THE ARTISTS

CHARLES VESS *(cover)*, born in 1951, is best known as the illustrator of *Blueberry Girl* and *Instructions* by Neil Gaiman as well as *The Cats of Tanglewood Forest* and *Seven Wild Swans* by Charles de Lint. Although he doesn't usually remember his dreams, he sometimes wakes up in the midst of telling himself a story complete with plot, character, and dialogue. WWW.GREENMANPRESS.COM

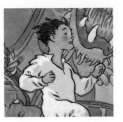

PETER DIAMOND *(page 4)*, born in 1981, is best known for his illustrations in *The Howler*, *The Progressive*, *The National Post*, and *The New York Times*. His dreams are often collages of the neighborhoods in the various cities where he has lived. WWW.PETERDIAMOND.CA

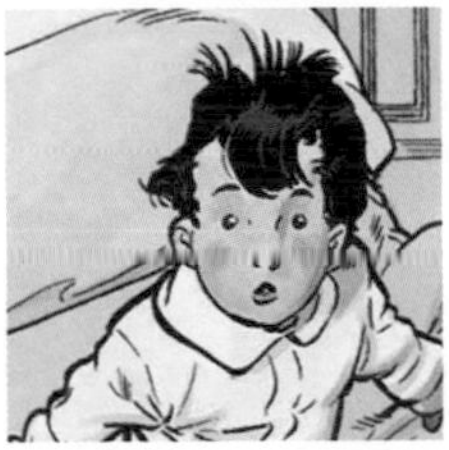

MARK BUCKINGHAM *(page 5)*, born in 1966, is best known for his art on the comic series *Marvelman* and *Fables*. He wishes he had time to dream but only has recurring nights of long hours working at his drawing board.

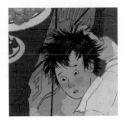

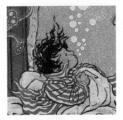

YUKO SHIMIZU *(page 14)* is best known for her cover art for the comic series *The Unwritten* and her illustrations for *Time*, *Newsweek*, and *The New Yorker*. She doesn't usually remember her dreams, so she uses art to create dreamscapes instead. WWW.YUKOART.COM

OH! OH! NO MORE MELTED CHEESE FOR ME, MAMA!

ROGER LANGRIDGE *(page 17)*, born in 1967, is best known for his comic series *Fred the Clown* and as the writer and artist of *The Muppet Show* comic book series. As a kid, he dreamed that he lost his mother in a frightening shopping mall, and when he found her, she had no facial features, just a blur where they should have been. WWW.HOTELFRED.COM

OPEN UP!

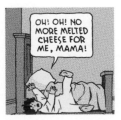

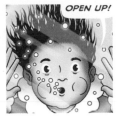

PETER AND MARIA HOEY *(page 19)*, born in 1960 and 1973, are a brother-and-sister team best known for their independent comic press, Coin-Op Books. Peter sometimes dreams that it's twilight, and he's back somewhere he used to live, with a dark blue sky, and dark shadows running across streets and up the sides of buildings. Maria sometimes has scary dreams and wakes up shouting "Get away!" or "Help!" WWW.COINOPBOOKS.COM

A DREAM.

PAOLO RIVERA *(page 21)*, born in 1981, is best known for his art on the comic series *Daredevil*, *Amazing Spider-Man*, and *Mythos*. He sometimes dreams that it's the zombie apocalypse and he has to fortify his parents' house and build rooftop walkways in his hometown of Daytona Beach. WWW.PAOLORIVERA.COM

THERE! IF YOU MUST BITE, YOU CAN SLEEP ON THE FLOOR!

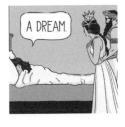

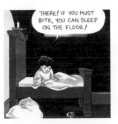

CARLA SPEED MCNEIL *(page 23)*, born in 1969, is best known for her comic series *Finder*. When she was in college, she dreamed she was falling through a brilliant blue sky and felt as if she would keep falling forever. WWW.LIGHTSPEEDPRESS.COM

ANOTHER BAD DREAM, WINSOR?
NO... A GOOD ONE. BUT I FEEL LIKE I'VE BEEN ASLEEP FOR A VERY LONG TIME.
I'LL GO MAKE THE COFFEE.

CLIFF CHIANG *(page 25)*, born in 1974, is best known for his art on the *Wonder Woman* series. As a kid, he used to dream about being in the bath and eating a giant cookie. WWW.CLIFFCHIANG.COM

I TOLD YOU TO PUT YOUR LEGOS AWAY.
OW

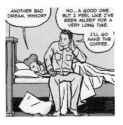

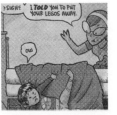

ZANDER CANNON *(page 27)*, born in 1972, is best known for his art on the comic series *Top 10* and *Smax*. He once dreamed he was in the atrium of a Victorian hotel with an old and labyrinthine elevator system. WWW.BARRELMAG.COM

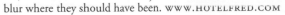

CRAIG THOMPSON *(page 29)*, born in 1975, is best known for the books *Blankets* and *Habibi* as well as the kids' comic *Space Dumplins* (Fall 2015). He sometimes has dreams about praying mantises fusing together to become a mega mantis monster.
WWW.DOOTDOOTGARDEN.COM

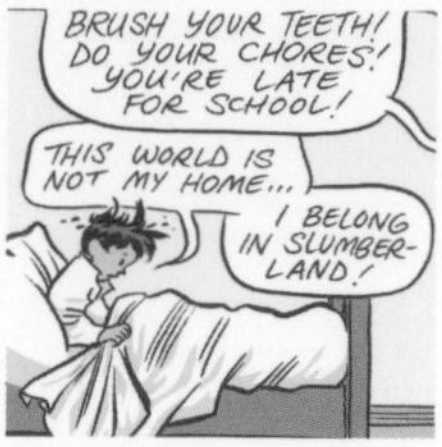
BRUSH YOUR TEETH! DO YOUR CHORES! YOU'RE LATE FOR SCHOOL!
THIS WORLD IS NOT MY HOME...
I BELONG IN SLUMBERLAND!

JAMIE TANNER *(page 41)*, born in 1976, is best known for his books *The Aviary* and *The Black Well.* Although he doesn't usually remember his dreams, as a child he once sleepwalked through the house shouting: "I don't wanna play with Rambo!" WWW.JAMIETANNER.COM

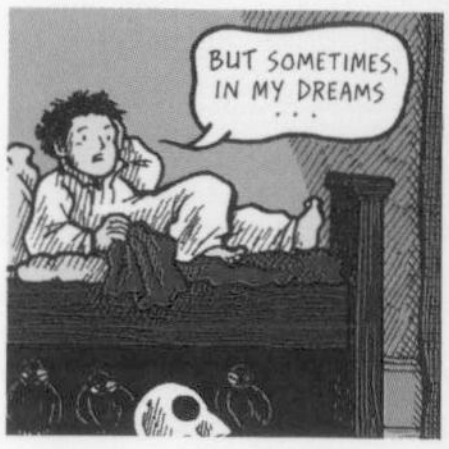
BUT SOMETIMES, IN MY DREAMS . . .

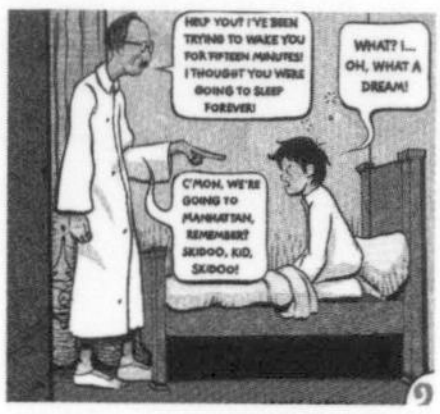
HELP YOU? I'VE BEEN TRYING TO WAKE YOU FOR FIFTEEN MINUTES! I THOUGHT YOU WERE GOING TO SLEEP FOREVER!
WHAT? I... OH, WHAT A DREAM!
C'MON, WE'RE GOING TO MANHATTAN, REMEMBER? SKIDOO, KID, SKIDOO!

JAMES HARVEY *(page 31)*, born in 1983, is best known for editing the global collaborative project *Bartkira* and for his short story "Masterplasty." He once dreamed that America was about to capsize into the Atlantic.
WWW.STOPJAMESHARVEY.COM

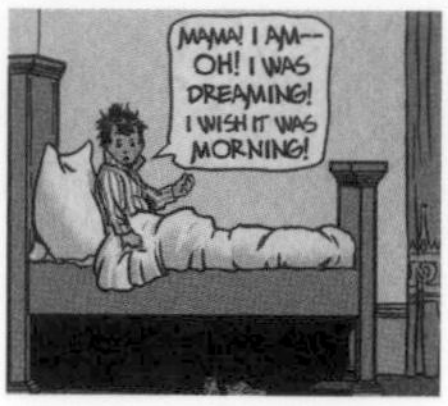
MAMA! I AM-- OH! I WAS DREAMING! I WISH IT WAS MORNING!

NIK POLIWKO *(page 43)* is best known as the artist on Edgar Rice Burroughs's *The War Chief* comic strip. He once dreamed that he was flying at great speed through vast mountains and canyons in the Canadian Arctic.
WWW.POLIWKO.WORDPRESS.COM

DAVID MACK *(page 33)*, born in 1972, is best known for his comic series *Kabuki* and as a writer for the *Daredevil* series. He often has dreams about flying.
WWW.DAVIDMACK.COM

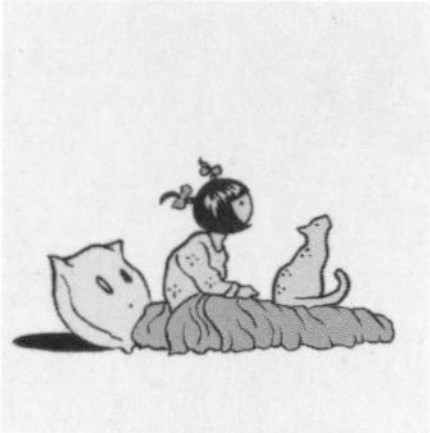

DAVID PLUNKERT *(page 45)*, born in 1965, is best known for his poster art, his comic series *Heroical*, and the book, *Edgar Allan Poe: Stories & Poems.* He sometimes has dreams about walking in a concrete maze lodged in a desolate hillside.
WWW.DAVIDPLUNKERT.COM

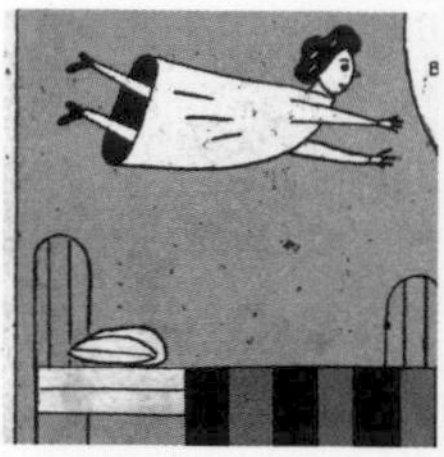

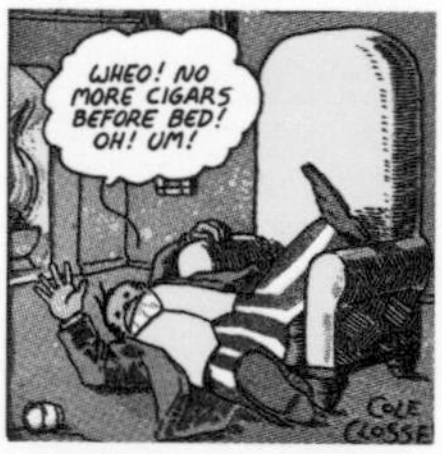
WHEO! NO MORE CIGARS BEFORE BED! OH! UM!

COLE CLOSSER *(page 35)*, born in 1980, is the author of *Little Tommy Lost.* He has a lot of adventure dreams—swashbuckling, spaceships, chases, and close calls. He also dreams about empty houses with dark rooms and enormous windows.
WWW.COLECLOSSER.COM

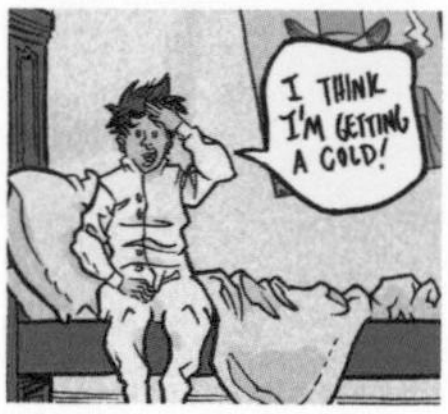
I THINK I'M GETTING A COLD!

AARON M. CONLEY *(page 47)*, born in 1977, is best known for the book *Sabertooth Swordsman.* He once had a dream that Mike Mignola called him on the phone to ask if he knew how to draw a futuristic treadmill.
WWW.INVADEMYPRIVACY.COM

JEREMY A. BASTIAN *(page 37)*, born in 1978, is the author of *Cursed Pirate Girl.* He sometimes has dreams that he's in the toy aisle of a grocery store and finds a hidden cache of old G.I. Joe figures and then wakes up really disappointed.
WWW.ARTOFJEREMYBASTIAN.COM

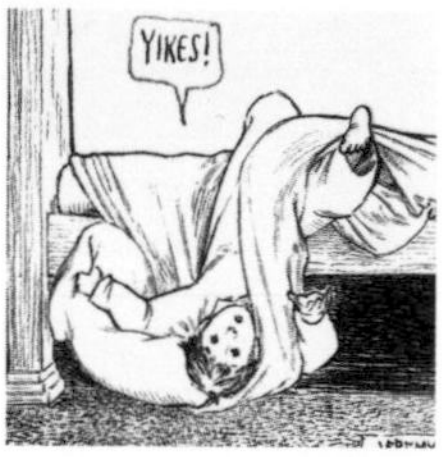
YIKES!

BISHAKH KUMAR SOM *(page 49)*, born in 1968, is best known for his comics in *Hi-horse, Blurred Vision, Pood, Specs,* and the *Graphic Canon* series. He sometimes dreams that he is in the audience at a Judas Priest concert watching the lead singer fly above the audience singing an imaginary song called "You'll Never Know How Hard I Rock and Roll."
WWW.BISHAKH.COM

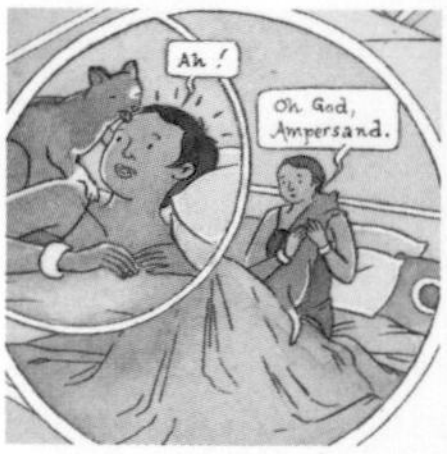
Ah!
Oh God, Ampersand.

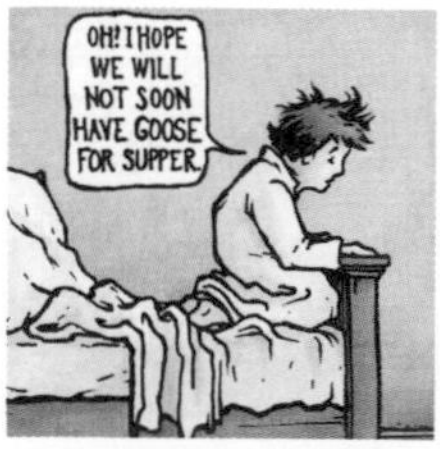
OH! I HOPE WE WILL NOT SOON HAVE GOOSE FOR SUPPER.

DAVID PETERSEN *(page 39)*, born in 1977, is best known for his comic series *Mouse Guard.* As a child, he used to dream about discovering a secret room in his attic that had antique toys, books, and friends who were waiting for him.
WWW.MOUSEGUARD.NET

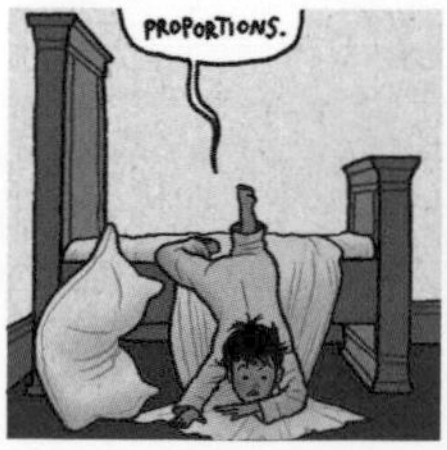
PROPORTIONS.

MARIS WICKS/JOE QUINONES *(page 51)* Maris is the author of *Primates: The Fearless Science of Jane Goodall, Dian Fossey, and Birute Galdikas* and is known for her work on *Spongebob Comics.* She sometimes dreams about swimming contentedly with sharks. WWW.DOTSFOREYES.COM.
Joe is best known for his art on *Black Canary & Zatanna* and the upcoming *Howard the Duck.* He sometimes dreams about being hunted by monsters. WWW.JOEQUINONES.NET

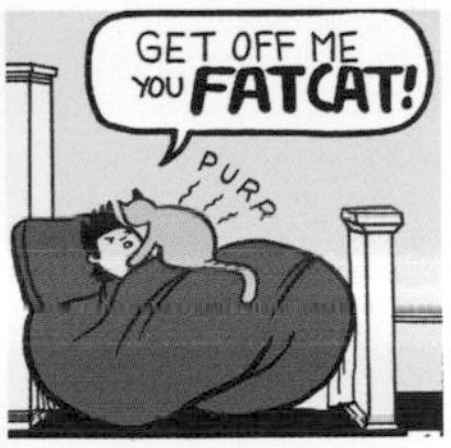
GET OFF ME YOU FATCAT!
PURR

BOX BROWN *(page 53)*, born in 1980, is the author of *Andre the Giant: Life and Legend* and the founder of the publishing house Retrofit Comics. Lately he has been having dreams about being so frustrated that he smashes and destroys his possessions.
WWW.BOXBROWN.COM

ANDREA TSURUMI *(page 55)*, born in 1985, is best known for her illustrations in *The New York Times*, *Boston Globe*, *The Nib*, and the *Graphic Canon* series. She once had a dream that she was surrounded by wombats and got annoyed because they took up too much room.
WWW.ANDREATSURUMI.COM

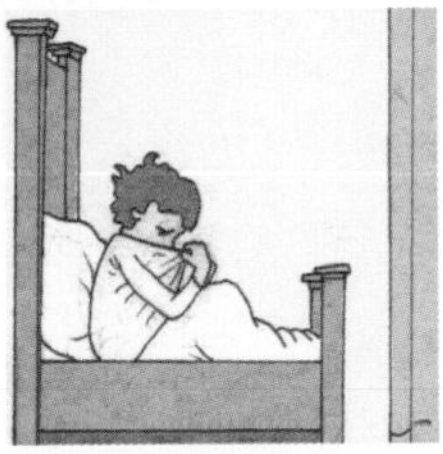

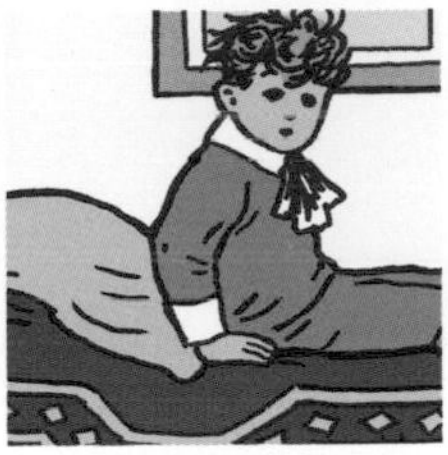

R. SIKORYAK *(page 57)* was born in 1964. He is the author of *Masterpiece Comics* and many other books. After spending long hours at the computer, he sometimes dreams that he is still staring at the screen and tweaking details of his drawing.
WWW.RSIKORYAK.COM

HANS RICKHEIT *(page 59)*, born in 1973, is best known for his books *Chloe* and *The Squirrel Machine* and for the webcomics *Cochlea & Eustachia* and *Ectopiary*. Most of his comics are based on his dreams.
WWW.CHROMEFETUS.COM

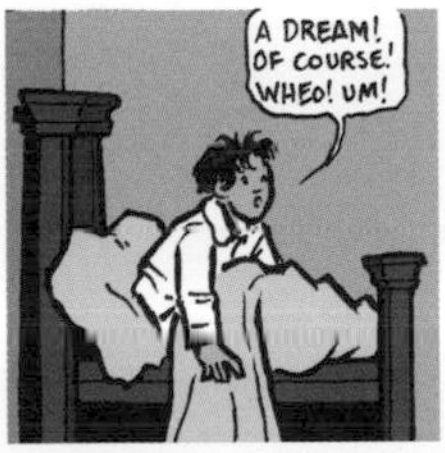
A DREAM! OF COURSE! WHEO! UM!

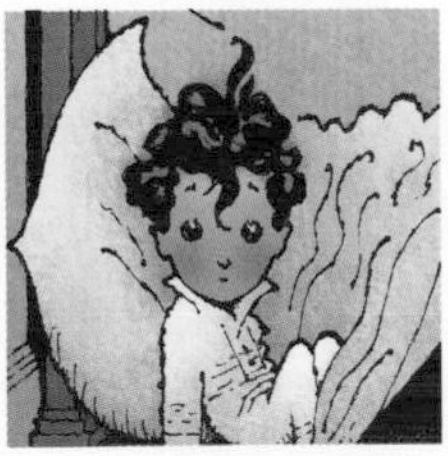

MARC HEMPEL *(page 61)*, born in 1957, is best known for his work on *The Sandman: The Kindly Ones* and his humor series *Gregory* and *Tug & Buster*. He once dreamed that he was visiting his grandparents' house and suddenly noticed a swimming pool in the living room.
WWW.MARCHEMPEL.NET

JAMES YANG *(page 62)* is the author of the children's books *Joey and Jet* and *Puzzlehead*. He sometimes dreams about taking a running start, jumping into the air, and flying. WWW.JAMESYANG.COM

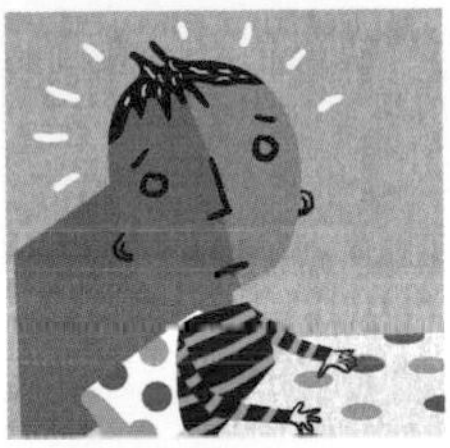

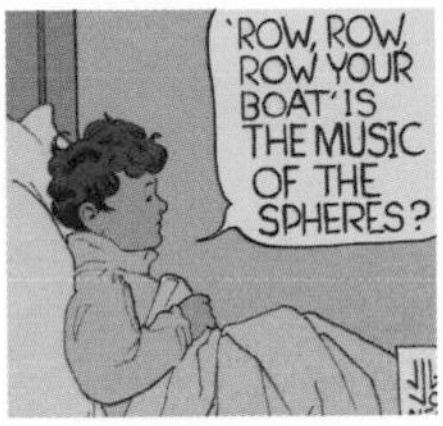
'ROW, ROW, ROW YOUR BOAT' IS THE MUSIC OF THE SPHERES?

J.G. JONES *(page 63)* is best known for his art on the comic series *Wanted*, *Final Crisis*, and *Before Watchmen: Comedian*. He can't remember any of his dreams.

JIM RUGG *(page 66)*, born in 1977, is best known for his books *Street Angel* and *Afrodisiac* and as the artist for the young adult comic book *The PLAIN Janes*. When he was in college, he used to dream the he could fly and that it felt a bit like gliding. WWW.JIMRUGG.COM

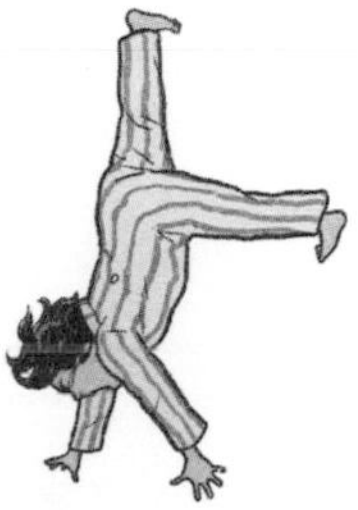

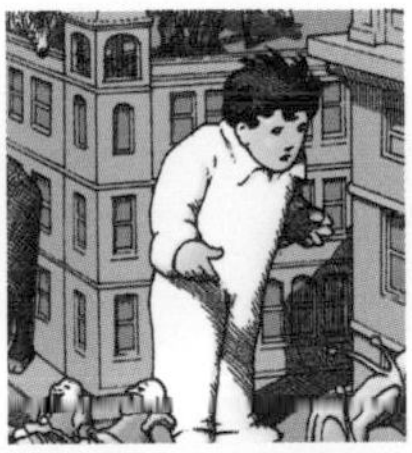

GERHARD *(back cover)*, born in 1959, is best known as the co-illustrator and co-publisher of *CEREBUS*. He sometimes dreams about sailing the clear blue waters of Georgian Bay in Ontario, Canada (which he also does in real life).
WWW.GERHARDART.COM

ZENAS WINSOR McCAY was born in Spring Lake, Michigan, but there are no official records of when–it could have been any year from 1867 to 1871. His obituary in the *New York Herald Tribune* stated, "not even Mr. McCay knew his exact age." He died in 1934.

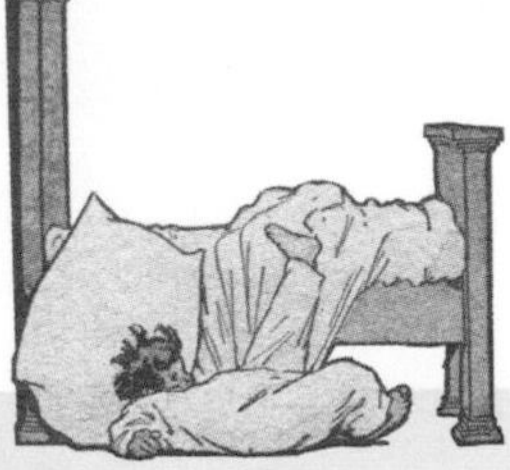

SELECTED BIBLIOGRAPHY

LITTLE NEMO: DREAM ANOTHER DREAM; Edited by Josh O'Neill, Andrew Carl, and Chris Stevens. Locust Moon Press, 2014. *The full version of this book. A large-size collection of contemporary strips inspired by Little Nemo.*

LITTLE NEMO IN SLUMBERLAND: SO MANY SPLENDID SUNDAYS!; Winsor McCay. Edited by Peter Maresca. Sunday Press, 2005. *The first of two full-scale reprints. A favorite with comics fans and an inspiration for the Locust Moon book.*

THE COMPLETE LITTLE NEMO; Winsor McCay. Edited by Alexander Braun. Taschen, 2014. *A large, single-volume collection of all 549 strips.*

THE COMPLETE LITTLE NEMO IN SLUMBERLAND (VOL 1-6); Winsor McCay. Fantagraphics, 1998-2014. *The Little Nemo adventures in six volumes.*

LITTLE SAMMY SNEEZE; Winsor McCay. Edited by Peter Maresca. Sunday Press, 2007. *McCay's first comic strip, about a boy with disastrous sneezes.*

DREAMS OF A RAREBIT FIEND: THE SATURDAYS; Winsor McCay. Checker Book, 2006. *McCay's black and white strips about eating too much melted cheese before bed.*

WIDE AWAKE IN SLUMBERLAND: FANTASY, MASS CULTURE, AND MODERNISM IN THE ART OF WINSOR MCCAY; Katherine Roeder. University Press of Mississippi, 2014. *An analysis of McCay's work through the lens of art history.*

WINSOR MCCAY: HIS LIFE AND ART; John Canemaker. Abrams Books, 2005. *The definitive biography of McCay.*

WINSOR MCCAY: THE MASTER EDITION (DVD); Winsor McCay, John Canemaker. Image Entertainment, 2004. *McCay's early animations and a documentary about the artist.*

Online Resources:
WWW.GOCOMICS.COM/LITTLE-NEMO *Sunday Press offers the full collection of Nemo Sunday pages.*

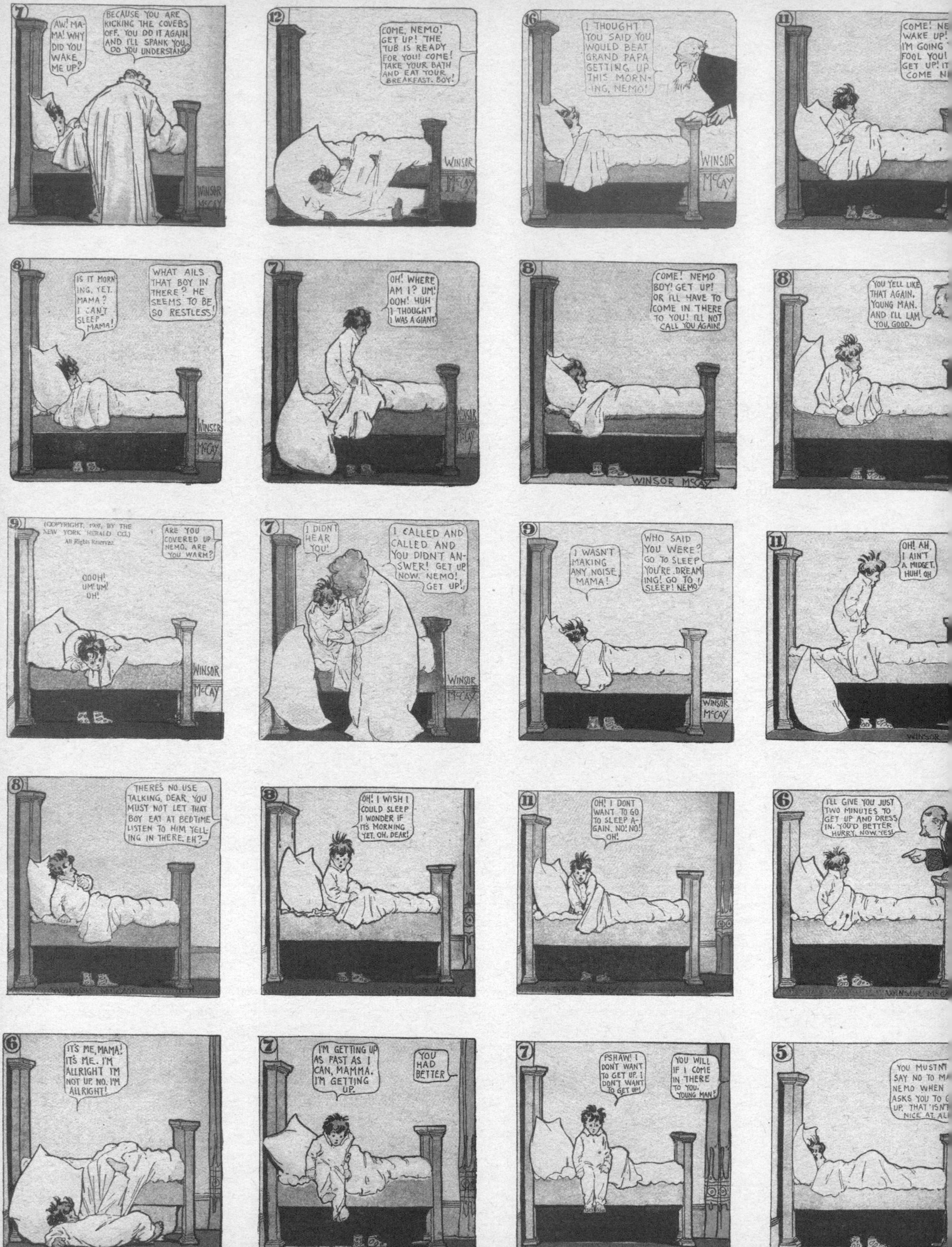
7
AW! MA-MA! WHY DID YOU WAKE ME UP?
BECAUSE YOU ARE KICKING THE COVERS OFF. YOU DO IT AGAIN AND I'LL SPANK YOU. DO YOU UNDERSTAND?
WINSOR McCAY
12
COME, NEMO! GET UP! THE TUB IS READY FOR YOU! COME! TAKE YOUR BATH AND EAT YOUR BREAKFAST, BOY!
WINSOR McCAY
16
I THOUGHT YOU SAID YOU WOULD BEAT GRAND PAPA GETTING UP THIS MORNING, NEMO!
WINSOR McCAY
11
COME! NE WAKE UP! I'M GOING FOOL YOU! GET UP! IT COME N
8
IS IT MORNING, YET. MAMA? I CAN'T SLEEP MAMA!
WHAT AILS THAT BOY IN THERE? HE SEEMS TO BE SO RESTLESS!
WINSOR McCAY
7
OH! WHERE AM I? UM! OOH! HUH I THOUGHT I WAS A GIANT!
WINSOR McCAY
8
COME! NEMO BOY! GET UP! OR I'LL HAVE TO COME IN THERE TO YOU! I'LL NOT CALL YOU AGAIN!
WINSOR McCAY
8
YOU YELL LIKE THAT AGAIN, YOUNG MAN, AND I'LL LAM YOU, GOOD.
9
(COPYRIGHT, 1907, BY THE NEW YORK HERALD CO.) All Rights Reserved.
ARE YOU COVERED UP NEMO, ARE YOU WARM?
OOOH! UM! UM! OH!
WINSOR McCAY
7
I DIDN'T HEAR YOU!
I CALLED AND CALLED AND YOU DIDN'T ANSWER! GET UP NOW, NEMO! GET UP!
WINSOR McCAY
9
I WASN'T MAKING ANY NOISE, MAMA!
WHO SAID YOU WERE? GO TO SLEEP YOU'RE DREAMING! GO TO SLEEP! NEMO!
WINSOR McCAY
11
OH! AH, I AIN'T A MIDGET, HUH! OH
WINSOR
8
THERE'S NO USE TALKING, DEAR, YOU MUST NOT LET THAT BOY EAT AT BEDTIME LISTEN TO HIM YELLING IN THERE, EH?
8
OH! I WISH I COULD SLEEP I WONDER IF IT'S MORNING YET. OH, DEAR!
11
OH! I DON'T WANT TO GO TO SLEEP AGAIN. NO! NO! OH!
6
I'LL GIVE YOU JUST TWO MINUTES TO GET UP AND DRESS IN. YOU'D BETTER HURRY, NOW, YES!
WINSOR McCAY
6
IT'S ME, MAMA! IT'S ME. I'M ALLRIGHT I'M NOT UP. NO. I'M ALLRIGHT!
7
I'M GETTING UP AS FAST AS I CAN, MAMMA. I'M GETTING UP.
YOU HAD BETTER
7
PSHAW! I DON'T WANT TO GET UP. I DON'T WANT TO GET UP!
YOU WILL IF I COME IN THERE TO YOU, YOUNG MAN!
WINSOR McCAY
5
YOU MUSTN'T SAY NO TO MA NEMO WHEN ASKS YOU TO G UP. THAT ISN'T NICE AT AL